YOU ARE MY WORLD

YOU ARE MY WORLD

Rheta Dewberry Norman

Library of Congress Control Number: 2022910045
ISBN: Hardcover   978-1-6698-0732-2
                   Softcover   978-1-6698-0731-5
                   eBook   978-1-6698-0730-8

Print information available on the last page.

Rev. date: 05/25/2022

To order additional copies of this book, contact:
Xlibris
844-714-8691
www.Xlibris.com
Orders@Xlibris.com
836044

CHAPTER 1

Monday afternoon November 17

MARY ELIZABETH

Sixty year old Mary stood in the picture window of her ranch style home and looked at the snow coming down like feathers from the sky. She was glad she had run all her errands and done all her grocery shopping early that morning before the roads got bad. She worried about people being out in this kind of weather. Even though she loved winter, she was not one to try to do much maneuvering in bad weather. As she turned from the window, the television newsman said they could be in for a week of snow and ice.

Just then, she saw a red blur out of the corner of her eye and she quickly turned, thinking that a child riding his bike might be skidding into the intersection. But what she saw as a tiny red sport car skidding in circles. Luckily there were no cars parked on the street. The car came to a stop in a snow bank across the street that nearly covered the back end of it. Slowly, a huge man got out and slid around the back to take a look at the car. He started digging in the snow around the back tires, trying to get them out. He got in the car and tried to drive it but the tires were just spinning around getting deeper in the snow. He got out again and rocked it from side to side and back to forth, but the car would not budge. In sheer frustration, he got in the car and tried to dislodge it once again. He apparently called someone and intended to wait for them to pick him up.

Poor fellow, Mary thought as she walked away from the window feeling bad for the big man and his little red car. She put on the teakettle for another cup of lemon mint tea. Looking back at the window, the man was still trying to dig his tires out of the snow with his hands. He stopped, looking around for some help.

He headed to the vacant house across from his car and knocked loudly on the door. He waited and didn't bother to knock again. Instead, he went next door to the Hemphills' house which was also empty. They were in Florida, visiting their son and his family. He then came across the street and tried the house next door to Mary. The Sheltons' were also away for the winter. They were in Mexico at their summer home. He came into Mary's yard. He looked even bigger than he did when he was across the street. He looked more like a giant than a man. He raised his fist to knock and she opened the door. She must have definitely startled him.

"I think you could use a little help," she said smiling. He tried to speak but he was shaking so badly by then, he could only nod his head. He wore a gray cashmere coat, matching hat and black leather gloves which were all covered with snow and soaking wet like his feet encased in wet black wingtip shoes. Looking at his expensive car and the clothes he wore, money was probably not a problem for him.

She opened the door wider and he slowly walked in. He was acting like he was in shock or something. She peeled his wet gloves off his hands and led him into the living room where she reached for his coat and hat. While he was removing his coat and hat, she went to the kitchen and threw some clean dishtowels in the microwave. He handed his coat and hat to Mary and slowly sat down.

The microwave shut off and she hurried to get the towels and quickly wrapped some around his hands. She knelt in front of him and unlaced his shoes. She looked up briefly into the saddest but the most beautiful eyes she had ever seen. They were amber like the color of honey. She eased his shoes and socks off and dried his feet with some paper towels. She wrapped the remaining warm towels around them. She felt a jolt of something like electricity shoot through her body when she barely touched the skin on his feet. They both felt that jolt because they both jumped. What on earth was that? Mary didn't give it much thought but she did notice it and she wouldn't forget it because it had never happened before, whatever it was. And there was certainly no static electricity built up by her kneeling and wrapping his hands and feet. It was a strange happening, but they pretended that it never happened.

The man closed his eyes and whispered so softly that Mary could barely hear him, "Thank you, Jesus, for this Angel.....ahh."

"Better?" She asked.

"Yes and thank you so much. I suspect I was pretty close to having frost bitten hands and feet if you hadn't been here. Not to mention going into shock. It is freezing cold out there."

She heard the teakettle so she got up from the floor and went to make them both a cup of tea. He was still shaking but not like before. He held the hot mug pretty steady considering his hands were wrapped in dishtowels. He took a sip of the hot liquid and closed his eyes again.

Mary took this opportunity to take a closer look at this giant of a man. He was the color of caramel candy with a bald head. His complexion was clear and his skin was smooth. He had a dimple in his chin and his mustache was neat and as white as snow. He was very handsome, Mary thought, like a model in the ads in her AARP magazine. Yum Yum! What a good looking man.

He had to be at least six feet five because Mary's grandson Karl is six feet even and he's much taller than Karl. What on earth was he doing on Harold Street on a day like this? He must have gotten lost.

Mary introduced herself and the man introduced himself. He is the Michael David Scott who is always in the society pages of the newspaper. Mary remembers seeing him quite often in the business section of the paper also. She knew one thing for sure. The pictures in the paper did not do him justice. He was a big piece of eye candy that looked good from every angle!

MICHAEL

Well, Michael thought to himself, he should thank God again that his hostess at least reads the paper or watches the news on TV and knew who he was. At least she had heard his name before today. Otherwise, he may not have gotten in the door. But this Mary Elizabeth Cross is some kind of special woman. Very few women he knew would have wrapped a stranger's feet in her clean dishtowels!! He couldn't think of any woman who would have done such a thing. He was still stunned by her kindness. He would never forget what she had done for him; or how she had done it.

When she was wrapping his feet she barely touched him and he felt an electric current run through his entire body from his feet to his head and down to his fingers. He knew she felt it too, because they simultaneously jumped ever so slightly. Michael didn't have a clue as to what that meant, but he knew this woman had his full attention. He also knew that the shock when their skin touched really had him wondering what he had walked into.

Mary was about 5 feet tall and 135 pounds of luscious mocha chocolate with curves in all the right places; she had beautiful shiny silver hair that she wore in a short curly natural hair style. Her complexion was flawless and her smile was radiant and real. She had beautiful teeth and her lips looked perfect for kissing. She moved with graceful motions; watching her was like watching someone floating on ice. He really enjoyed watching her move; she moved around in her kitchen preparing their meal like a ballerina. The sway of her perfect rear end, had him undressing her while she cooked. He was very surprised at himself for thinking about this angel of a woman in such sensual terms, but the woman had a body that made his mind automatically want to do things to her. It had been a long time and after all, he was a man.

He was still awe struck by the fact that she had blackberry cobbler. It is his favorite all time dessert aside from fried pies which no one made any more. How can this be?

He was beginning to wonder whether God was trying to tell him something. He wasn't sure if he believed in fate, but he felt like his life was about to be turned upside down and in a good way. He was glad he didn't have to try to explain how he was feeling to anyone at the moment, because he couldn't. It was a feeling of joy and peace but he didn't know why.

They sat down to eat in record time, and he was amazed at how delicious the food was. Although it was simple, it was filling and very satisfying. He did hear himself moan a couple of times during the meal. It was absolutely outstanding. He hoped he remembered to ask for the recipe for his parents' cook. The cornbread literally melted in his mouth and it didn't even need the mound of butter he put on it. He ate two bowls of soup and had three pieces of cornbread. Then he remembered the cobbler.

Just about the time he was going to say how he wished he had some vanilla ice cream, she rose from the table to get the cobbler. He didn't know that he actually saw what he was looking at because she reentered the room carrying two bowls of cobbler topped with vanilla ice cream. It took all he had not to jump up and kiss this angel of a woman.

"Damn, I mean, Gosh. Oh my! What an absolutely wonderful surprise.

Here I was wishing for some ice cream and ▮▮ of a sudden it appears before my eyes. How did you know?" he i▮▮▮d as he took his bowl of dessert from her hand. His eyes probably looked like those of a little boy on Christmas morning. He wondered if she k▮▮w how easy it was to make him happy – just some blackberry cobbler w▮▮ ▮anilla ice cream on the top.

"Well, it just happens to be how I ▮ to serve my cobbler. It's a southern thing I guess." She informed ▮▮▮.

"Where and when did you get your first taste of blackberry cobbler? I didn't take you for a southerner. Thought you were born and bred right here in Hartford."

The cobbler was slowly disappearing from his bowl. He was savoring each bite, so it didn't disappear as quickly as the soup.

He sat back and looked her in the eye, and smiled dreamily and said, "That brought back memories of Leesville, Georgia, back when I was a boy spending time in the country with my Uncle Ben and Aunt Frankie. They had a cook who made cobbler that tasted just like yours. Her name was Ruth. Boy, that woman could cook. I loved her a lot. I think about her sometimes and wonder where she is and whether she's still alive. I cannot count the number of times she saved me and my cousins from my aunt's switches. She saved us just about every day."

As Mike remembered those hot summer days in Georgia he thought about his cousin Red. He is a district judge in Madison, Wisconsin, a far cry from the sandy haired boy throwing rotten fruit on old man Phillips' porch. They were always coming up with something to do that would get them a good switching if they got caught.

Michael finally finished his cobbler and ice cream. He was so full he didn't think he could move from the table. Mary offered him coffee and all he could do was nod. He knew that was impolite but he was just that full. He decided he wanted both recipes before he left that house; the soup and the cobbler.

Mary took a tray with their coffee into the living room where they settled down to watch television. The programs kept being interrupted with weather advisories asking people to stay off the roads and be sure to bring their pets inside.

After a very pleasant few hours of watching programs that she liked, and only talking during the commercials, he found out that this Mary was a Christian woman who had been widowed more than twenty years. She had three married children and 8 grandchildren who all lived close enough to get to her within an hour or so if she needed them. She obviously loved them and they were all planning to be here for Thanksgiving just like always.

Michael wished he could be there too. Not just for the food, but for the love and happiness and family togetherness that somehow he just knew would be in this house around the dining room table. Who knows, he might be invited back. But that was a couple of weeks from now. He first had to survive here tonight and most likely a few more nights without getting put out before he could think about being here Thanksgiving.

Mary showed him to his room where she had her grandson's PJs, robe and slippers laid out for him. She showed him the towels and extra blankets. She asked him if there was anything else he needed, and his gut reaction told him to snatch her up and toss her on the bed and say, 'not anymore.' But he just smiled and said he would be fine. He thanked her again for her hospitality and she smiled and told him he was welcome. She floated out the door and closed it softly.

Michael thought maybe something was off. She was too nice. Or was it just him? Was it that he was so used to paying for everything he got, he couldn't recognize kindness without expectations when it was shown to him?

This woman had not been made nor asked to do anything for him. But she opened her home to him and saved him from frost bite; and fed him the most delicious home cooked meal he had had in years, and she expected nothing in return. Some people were kind by nature. Other than his mother, and Mama Ruth, he didn't think he had ever met one. He often wondered where she was, his Mama Ruth.

She worked for his uncle and aunt in Georgia when he was a boy. He and his cousins spent every summer down in the country with Mama Ruth cooking and keeping them out of trouble. They had chores to do and they had better be done before asking to go anywhere or do anything. She didn't mind giving them her fly swatter on their legs and behinds when they tried to get out of hand. She was so sweet, kind and full of love for all of the Scotts. In a funny sort of way, Mary sort of reminded Michael of Mama Ruth. They were both genuine, not fakes. Michael liked that about Mary and he really wanted to know more about her. He knew she did not have a problem speaking her mind, and she also believed in raising children to be independent and to not be needy or greedy.

Michael prepared for bed and his thoughts stayed on his angel. He thought about how she moved; the way her body was shaped and all the curves and how soft he knew she would feel; how he wanted to get her in his bed or vice versa.

Then he thought about how he effortlessly and ever so slowly began to enjoy her company without even noticing her face or her body. Boy, life sure has a way of making course corrections in the middle of a stream. Not that he had any particular standard that he used when selecting a lady companion, he just usually went for women who were slender and tall. They usually wore lots of make-up and had a lot of fake body parts. They had the boobs, the injected booty, hair extensions and weaves and wigs; not to mention long eyelashes, and colored contacts, and long fake nails. One thing was for certain – Mary Elizabeth Cross was real, there wasn't a fake thing about her from head to toe that he could see. Knowing this made him smile.

He settled in this big comfy queen sized bed with linen that smelled like spring rain with just a touch of lilac. Another fragrance he will never forget. He drifted off to sleep thinking about his angel and how blessed, not lucky, he really was. He was eagerly looking forward to what tomorrow would bring.

MARY ELIZABETH

While Mary was putting up the dishes, she thought back to how delighted Michael was with the meal. It was only soup, cornbread and cobbler, but you would have thought she served prime rib! 'What would he do if I actually planned a special meal just for him?' she wondered.

She would love to surprise him and see the look on his face after he tasted one of her favorite meals, steak and potatoes. Maybe she would get to surprise him one day. Then she thought, that didn't make sense since he already had a cook. Mary was sure steak and potatoes were something he ate all the time. You never know she thought; hers could be more memorable than other ones he's had.

She called Mama Lou to see if she was still up and she was, so Mary told her she was bringing some soup to the side door. She put on her jacket with the hood on it that she kept behind the door in the pantry. She went outside and stepped slowly and carefully until she made her way to Mama Lou's side door with her key ready to open the door when Mama

Lou opened it. She put her key back into her jacket pocket and entered the house.

"Wow, it is freezing outside!" she said as she handed Mama Lou the soup. She told her she couldn't stay but a minute because she had a house guest. Mama Lou said she had seen that big giant of a man going from door to door trying to get help with his car.

"Glad he finally got to you. Mighty handsome fellow too, isn't he? Maybe this is God sending you a man since to you won't go out anywhere so you can meet one on your own." That was Mary's cue to leave. Forever the matchmaker, she knew this was the real conversation Mama Lou wanted to have.

"Now you listen to me, Mary Elizabeth. He's driving a nice sports car, and he's tall, handsome and dressed like he has money. Don't you be foolish and act all holier than thou with this man. You be a woman and see what will happen. I know you are lonesome for male companionship. I know you ain't dead and dried up yet. Now mind you, I'm not telling you to go jump in bed with the man tonight, but I am telling you to remember he is a man. At least be approachable. Give the man a chance to get to know you. You just be yourself. If this is God's doing, that's all you have to be; yourself. You just be you and God will do the rest."

Mary hugged and kissed Mama Lou who was the mother she had not had in a very long time. She heard her and would heed her wise words. Just like she had done so many times over the past 20 years they had been neighbors. Mary had to admit that Mama Lou was right. She does miss being in the company of a man. She did miss male companionship. However, she trusted God and she believed God's word. She knew she couldn't entertain sexual thoughts about the giant. But it's not very easy to avoid the thoughts of being in Michael's arms when he's right there in the house, across the hall from her bed. But she had faith to believe that with God's help she would be alright.

She cautiously crossed the side yard back to her house. When she reached for the back door it was flung open and she came face to face with an angry giant in her kitchen, clad in pajama bottoms that looked like Capris on him and an open robe revealing a bare chest sprinkled with white curls. With his hands on his hips, he looked like a father about to scold a teenager for breaking curfew. She quickly came in the house and shut the door, turned back to him and he had not moved nor had he said a word. She took off her jacket and he took it from her and hung it on the back of a chair.

"I heard the back door and thought it might be a burglar. Where have you been without a hat or gloves or a heavy coat? Don't you know there's a winter storm out there? You might have fallen and I wouldn't have even known you were gone." He said angrily.

She was shocked at his angry tirade. What's more she was a little touched that he cared about her well-being. She got the teakettle off the stove and put water in it and set it back on the stove to boil. Michael went around the kitchen island and grabbed her and pulled her to him in a hug that was just tight enough. It warmed her to the bone. Actually, she almost melted in his arms. He was trembling when she looked up at him. That's when she realized she had actually truly frightened him. She moved out of his embrace and told him she went next door to check on her 90 year old neighbor; and that she took her some soup for tomorrow. She apologized for making him worry. She tried to reassure him that she was quite used to taking care of herself and that she was fine.

He took her hand and guided her to the living room where the embers of the fire burning in the fireplace were glowing and casting a soft golden light into the room. She sat on the sofa and he knelt in front of her and said very quietly, "Mary Elizabeth Cross, I am well aware that you are used to taking care of yourself and looking out for yourself. But tonight and for however long I'm here, *that* becomes my job, and I would appreciate it if you just let me know when you leave out of the house. I don't mean to sound bossy or like your personal manager or a husband or something. I'm just a man being a man, protecting the woman in my presence.

Right then, she felt the armor around her heart begin to loosen. He reached up and touched her face with the most incredibly soft touch she had felt in a very long time. Their lips came together for a brief second just as the teakettle whistled. Perfect timing. That must be God, Mary thought.

They stood almost simultaneously looking at each other. Silently they went back into the kitchen. She poured hot water over chamomile tea bags and he got the honey off the counter. After adding the honey they took their mugs back into the living room and sat side by side.

Words were not needed because they knew that something had happened just then. Something had changed between them. It felt like things were okay but not right. Neither knew what to say or where to go from there without sending the wrong message? Mary certainly didn't want to mess up and she got the feeling he didn't either. So they just sat and sipped their tea and looked at the dying embers of the fire while their insides warmed and the protection around their hearts began to slowly melt. The communication was nonverbal. Both had thoughts of what could be, and they declined to share them. It isn't necessary to always express your thoughts. Sometimes silence speaks louder than words.

MICHAEL
Tuesday, November 18

When he woke up, at first Michael didn't know where he was or how he got there, but he knew he had just had the best night's sleep he'd had in years. He stretched and then became aware of an aroma that smelled like coffee, bacon and biscuits. He quickly went to the bathroom, shaved, showered and dressed in some sweats he found folded on a chair in the room. His feet were bare except for a pair of socks because the slippers left for him were just too small. Much to his surprise the floor wasn't cold. When he got to the kitchen, Mary was sitting at the island and spoke, "Well, good morning, Michael. I hope you slept well."

He stared at his angel who looked even better today than she did yesterday. She had on black sweats with a long sleeved white t-shirt that had red, yellow and green Ghana written across the front. Her hair was in a perfect silver gray halo around her head. She wore a pair of gold and silver hoop earrings. No make-up but her skin looked so clear it glowed with good health.

"Good morning to you, Mary. You look pretty this morning." She had to hold herself back from coming over to him for a good morning kiss. She beckoned him to sit at the island and she got his plate ready with biscuits from the oven.

"I wondered what the time was and when I looked at the clock on the stove and saw it was 11:48, I didn't believe it." Michael said with that child-like look of surprise on his face.

He looked at her and she smiled. She told him she knocked on the bedroom door, and when she didn't get an answer, she came in and left him the sweats. That was around 7:30.

"In all my sixty-two years, I do not remember when or if I have ever slept past 9:00, even after being up all night. I don't believe I have ever slept this long in my life!"

He must have that look on his face because Mary said, "I guess the chamomile tea helped you relax. That's probably exactly what your body and mind needed, and you have probably needed it for a long time. Why not look at it like this, you don't have anything to do and you certainly can't go anywhere, so no harm was done." She was certainly right on both those counts.

He blessed his food and began to eat a breakfast of biscuits, bacon, cheese grits and scrambled eggs. It was wonderful and the coffee was perfect. He looked up at her and she was smiling. He smiled, nodded and went back to enjoying his breakfast or rather brunch. It was absolutely delicious! She left the kitchen and he could see her putting things on the dining room table.

Michael finished his meal, washed his dishes and put them in the dishwasher. He told Mary he had a briefcase in his car that he needed. She offered to get it for him, but he insisted on going himself. He made it to the door before he noticed his feet. Mary got his shoes which were dry and he put them on. He made it to the car without falling and then almost couldn't get the door open. He finally did and he got in and started the engine which purred to life right away. It was ready to take off, except the tires were still stuck in the snow. After he retrieved the briefcase and his phone charger, he slid back to the house where a cup of hot tea was waiting for him; and he appreciated very much.

He needed to do a little work, look over some documents and make some notes on some contracts. Mary took his phone and plugged it in her car in the garage. He looked around for someplace to spread his stuff and Mary offered him the dining room table. She said they could share it because that was where she was preparing to do her Bible study. He noticed she had two Bibles, a Bible dictionary, two Bible Concordances, her notebook and a box of colored pencils, pens, erasers and lead. Michael could see that she was a serious student of the Bible. He liked that.

After he settled down, with hot tea and a beautiful lady sharing his work space, he did a day's work in span of a few hours. He thought, 'I guess that's what peace and the sweet kindness of a beautiful woman will do for you. I am so in awe of my angel and all that makes her who she is.'

Mary ate a sandwich and he had some more soup for lunch. They talked about their lives and what they cared about. After listening to her talk about her love for God and His people, he understood why she was glowing. She has God's light shining through her and she's an earthly angel in every way - a real Christian. Not a pretend one, or not just one on Sundays, but a true Christian every day of the week!

Things she was involved with made his multi-million dollar deals seem so very minor. On Mondays, she does laundry for her neighbor and for herself, ran errands and did grocery shopping for both of them sometimes taking her neighbor with her.

She takes a water aerobics class on Monday, Wednesday and Friday mornings from 10-11am at the YWCA.

On Tuesday and Thursday, she volunteers at Connecticut Children's Medical Center 6 to 8 hours each week where she rocks, feeds and loves on the babies who need the human touch. She is that extra pair of hands for the nurses and where her service is invaluable. Her awards and certificates date back 14 years for her volunteer work at the Children's Medical Center.

On Wednesday, she reads stories at the neighborhood library from 12:00 noon until 1:30pm and from 2pm until 3:30pm.

On Thursday, she volunteers in the church bookstore from 11:30 am until 2pm.

On Friday morning she leads a Bible study class at St. Mary's Nursing Home 12:30pm-2:00pm.

She volunteers in the nursery on the third Sunday at the 11o'clock service. and she attends Bible Study on Thursday evenings. She also volunteers with a girls group on Saturday morning two or three times a year teaching abstinence.

Is she an angel or what? Michael was in awe of all she did. She is away from home a lot, but she somehow manages to keep her lovely home neat and clean. It's comfortable and not filled with knick knacks and other collectibles that often collect dust. It was the kind of home that made a person feel like taking their shoes off and staying awhile.

Michael decided that whatever she's taking, He wanted to buy it for some of his employees. Better yet, he figured he could fire his worst two and hire her to do their job and give her both salaries. He thought, 'I bet she could work rings around them and still have energy to burn!'

As they talked, they shared their dreams and he found hers to be fairly simple. She wants to make sure all her grands and any great-grands to come will have an opportunity to obtain a college education if they want one. She wants to give her daughters one piece of good jewelry. She wants to set-up a scholarship for the girls' organization she volunteers with at the church. Lastly, she wants to see some of the world that she has read about and seen pictures of in books.

Somewhere Michael heard a voice saying, "Mike, you have to see that her dreams come true." He suddenly got really drowsy, almost like he was drugged. He started hearing voices and day-dreaming about being in exotic places with this beautiful woman by his side.

Michael stretched, stood up and announced it was nap time. Mary smiled and stood too, looking up at him with those beautiful chocolate pools of warmth. He took her hand and they walked down the hall together.

When they reached the bedroom doors, she turned and looked up. He bent and their lips touched. She let out a moan which made him pull her closer to him so he could feel her soft body against him while he dipped his tongue into her delicious mouth. His hands cupped her luscious behind and he lifted her off her feet. She put her arms around his neck and kissed him back with a hunger that matched his own. She wrapped her legs around him and he leaned against the wall to balance himself. The kiss got deeper. He thought he was going to faint from the pleasure of it. Suddenly, he felt her go limp. He slowly let her down until her feet touched the floor. She leaned up against him trying to catch her breath. She felt his heart racing at the same pace as hers. She turned and entered her room and softly closed the door. Michael stayed leaning against the wall until his breathing returned to normal and he thought he could move without falling over.

When he entered his room he shut the door, fell across the bed and expected to instantly fall asleep. But his angel was circling around in his head. This woman was like a drug to him. He lost all sense of control when around her. 'This is getting scary,' he thought. 'Am I under a spell or is this what love feels like? It can't possibly be love because I have only known her one day, can it? Can it be God? God, I need to talk with You right now.'

'Oh God, speak through my heart to my head and tell me whether this is the woman You made for me. Please God; I need to hear from You. I am completely out of my element and I'm finding it hard to stay under control. I have never experienced these kinds of emotions or love for a woman. These feelings are so new and different for me. I know the kind of woman I am used to being with, and Mary Elizabeth Cross is definitely not that type. She is so sweet, real and so uncomplicated. She brings a breath of freshness into my life. She's not playing games, or trying to take me for whatever she can get. She's the opposite of what I am used to God, but she feels so right to me. She feels good in every kind of way. Is it her or is it just me being in a dry spell and grabbing at the first female in my path? Speak to my heart Lord Jesus.'

Michael drifted off to sleep with the sweet smell of Mary in his nostrils and the feel of her soft luscious body in his arms. He knows she is not a dream and yet how can she be real. She must be hiding something. He wished he could hide her in his arms right now. Mary Elizabeth Cross was making him crazy with desire and he was not used to denying himself. He wanted her but not just physically; he wanted the whole thing; all of her; heart, body and mind. Did he really? Or was he just after a good woman? Again he asked the Lord to help him because he didn't know what to do about what he as feeling right now.

MARY ELIZABETH

All night and all morning, Mary's thoughts returned to the almost kiss of she and Michael that first night. Their lips were so close. She could feel his breath on my lips. She wanted it and he did too. She wondered whether he could feel the change that she felt whenever they were near each other.

It has been so long since she had been in the company of a man. She was afraid she was a little rusty when it came to the little things women did to flirt these days. Mama Lou said to just be herself and be a woman, but how was she supposed to do that? Get up and put on make-up and a dress? That's not who she was and she never put on airs, no matter what. She had to be who she was. But, she had to admit, she was trying a little. She hoped she looked better today.

Speaking of morning, he's sleeping like he hasn't been to bed in weeks. She knocked on his door to tell him breakfast was ready and he didn't move. She could hear his steady breathing knew he was sleeping soundly. She left him some clean sweats, socks and slippers in his room. She stopped long enough to look at the beautiful, sweet man sleeping in her home. He was indeed a big man but he snored ever so softly.

She had hoped he would be up by now. It was almost eleven o'clock. Who knew executives slept so late? She expected him to fix breakfast and beat her getting up this morning just to be a show-off. Oh well, doesn't matter. He doesn't strike her as a man who knows very much about cooking anyway.

Today, she is going to do some Bible studying because she didn't want to get behind. She needed to study for the lesson she taught at the nursing home, although she didn't think they would be having class this week. She also had to be ready for her Thursday class at church whether they had class or not. She figured either way, she needed to continue her weekly study.

She knew what she was preparing for supper and she had already done all of the prep work she needed to do. Lunch was going to be leftovers. Now, if only he would get up. She spent the next 30 minutes talking to friends in her Bible study group at the nursing home.

She also spoke with her friends Lois and Billie from Shiloh Baptist. They talked about the weather and wondered how long the weather would keep them at home. All three of them laughed about the fact they were planners and "the ready girls" at Shiloh. They had everything they needed and weren't worried about having to leave the house. They asked about Mama Lou but they knew Mary was taking care of her. Mary didn't talk on the phone long. She wasn't the kind of person that stayed on the phone gossiping and talking about what was happening in the news.

As soon as she hung up from talking to her friends, her mind went straight to Michael Scott and the almost kiss. She kept thinking about him and wondering when he was getting up and suddenly she heard the shower. Shortly after that, just like she had summoned him with her mind, he came into the kitchen, and if it's possible, he looked even better than he did yesterday. She didn't know why but he just looked better. Maybe it had to do with the rest he had gotten.

He said good morning and then the next thing out of his mouth was, "You look pretty this morning." Mary couldn't believe it. She knew she blushed. All she could manage to say was thank you. She wanted to walk up to him and give him a good morning kiss. But instead, she motioned for him to sit at the island. When he noticed the time he was amazed, even shocked that it was almost noon. He said he didn't believe he had ever slept that long in his life and somehow, she believed him. He ate his breakfast and cleaned up the dishes when he finished and that was a pleasant surprise. Who knew rich people could do such ordinary things like wash their own dishes? Who knew he would even do it and not be asked to clean up behind himself. This was a special man, Mary thought to herself.

He got his brief case and came to the dining room to do some work. They sat on opposite ends of the table. He worked and she studied in silence for most of the afternoon with few interruptions. Mary's youngest daughter, Beverly, called to see if she alright. Later her oldest daughter, Karen, called to see if she needed anything. Alford, her first born called to see if her firewood was holding out and to check on Mama Lou.

They stopped for lunch and Michael was glad there was still some of that awesome soup and cornbread left from dinner. He graciously finished it off making sure there wouldn't be any leftovers after this meal. Mary ate a roast beef sandwich from her Sunday dinner.

They finally finished their work at the dining room table and moved to the sofa where they talked and had their dessert. They talked about their lives, their families, their hopes and their dreams. They talked like old friends. He did not believe Mary was 60. He had guessed her to be in her early 50s. She was just as surprised to learn that he was 62. She guessed him to be in his mid-50s. 'Oh well,' Mary thought, 'I guess we must be doing something right. I feel younger than my years, but I sure didn't think I *looked* younger than my years.' The idea that she looked that young sure made her feel good.

Michael told her that he is the only son of a grocery store owner and a librarian. He has several uncles and aunts and lots of cousins. His family is from Georgia. He finished high school in Hartford and went on to college. He graduated from Morehouse College, a private, all-male, liberal arts, historically black college in Atlanta. He liked talking about going to school without costing his parents anything but spending money. He had enough scholarships to take care of all of educational costs. He laughed and explained that back then, it was hard for his parents to send him spending money on a regular basis. He said he went sometimes weeks without a penny in his pocket. Because he didn't have money there wasn't much he could do outside of the campus so he spent a lot of time in the library. He also mentioned doing a lot of visiting at nearby Spelman College, the female equivalent of Morehouse. Apparently, the long hours he spent paid off in the long run. He graduated Summa Cum Laude and the doors of many Ivy League colleges and universities were open for him. He could choose which ever one he wanted to attend. He chose Yale in New Haven, Connecticut. He was grateful and ready to make his mark in the world.

Michael wanted to make his parents proud of him and it looks like he succeeded in doing that. He was always treating them to some of the better things in life. The things his father wouldn't take the time to enjoy when he was younger, now he can afford to go and do whatever and whenever he wants to now. But Michael insists on doing it for them. He always takes them on vacations, taking care of all the expenses. He takes them on a cruise at least once each year. They have been to Alaska and to the Bahamas, as well as visited several major cities in Europe and Asia. They are both in good health. They live in a cottage on Michael's property. He admitted that he spoils them. The more Mary learned, the more she saw that he really was a loving son and a good man.

Michael owns Scott Development Enterprises, a computer software company and MDS and Associates, an advertising and marketing company. He is into giving back to the community and he loves to help boys who don't have fathers in the home. Growing Boys to Men is a non-profit he founded that works with these boys from sixth grade until they graduate from high school.

He's not a member of any church, but he was reared Baptist. Mary didn't understand why he was not a member of any church. She knew he had a strong faith in God. She didn't ask him any questions about is non-affiliation with a church. She figured he had his reasons. She was itching to talk to him about it, but she kept her questions to herself. She hoped she could bring it up another time. She would love to see him become a member at Shiloh, but he would have to find his own church home.

He supports many youth oriented organizations and Mary didn't know how he found the time to keep up with everything. She decided his assistant must be as busy as he was since he helps him keep up with everything. His dream is to have a peaceful life without drama surrounded by people he loves and who love him. That's not such a hard dream to achieve. It's probably within reach right now, but he just can't see it because it doesn't look like what he has pictured in his mind. Well, only time will tell.

They stood to go to their rooms and he reached for her hand which she slipped in his as if they did it every day. When they got to their bedroom doors, Mary turned to him to say something and he kissed her. She morphed into someone else and completely, totally lost it. She kissed him back. At first it was a simple soft kiss but it turned into a kiss that had them both out of control. They kissed each other with the same fervor. Her lips burned from the intensity of the kiss. He lifted her off her feet and before she knew what happened, her legs were around his waist and her arms were around his neck. She didn't even know she could get her legs up like that! They continued to kiss until she thought she was going to faint. Michael pulled his mouth away and moaned at the same time she heard herself whimper. He slowly let her slide down the front of him. Her breasts were on fire as they slid down the hard muscles of his chest. When her feet touched the floor, they stood there in the hallway, holding on to each other, hearts beating to a silent tune and the same rhythm. She leaned into him to keep from falling because she knew her legs were like wet noodles at that moment. The only sound that could be heard by them was the duet being played by their hearts.

When she could move, she silently eased into her room, closed the door. She fell backwards onto the bed in total shock! What on earth had she just done? Where in the world did that come from? That was too much. She knew she couldn't do that again. This man was dangerous. He had her doing things that she didn't even know she could do! Things she had never, ever done before. Wow, what a man; what a kiss; what a problem; what a B-I-G problem. This was not good, although it certainly felt good. She was in trouble and she knew it. This thing that was growing between them was going to turn into a situation that would test her to her breaking point.

CHAPTER 2

Tuesday Evening, November 18

MARY ELIZABETH

Mary was not used to taking naps during the day and she didn't know why on earth she thought she could even walk down the hall with the giant. She knew the minute their hands touched something was going to happen. There was an energy surrounding them when they were in the same room that was so strong you could almost see it. She couldn't explain it, but she most definitely could feel it and she felt sure that Michael could feel it too.

Sure, she had an idea that the kiss would be potent, but she certainly hadn't anticipated that she would turn into an acrobat. She was still trying to figure out how she got her legs up around his waist with so little effort. If someone had told her she was capable of doing something that athletic, she would have laughed in their face. That move was simply unbelievable. It was as if her body had taken on a mind of its own. Not to mention the kiss! That kiss would be seared into her memory for all eternity. It was the deepest, longest, warmest, most sensuous kiss she ever had. It was way too much for her. Everything about it was too much. Kisses like that made her want to break her vow of celibacy and she just couldn't do that. Kisses like that should be restricted for only people who would follow it up with mind-blowing sex; and she couldn't do that either. It is simply impossible. Not physically impossible of course, but definitely of spiritually impossible.

So the taste of that kiss would have to last her a lifetime and she had no doubt that it would. Now she had to figure out how to get that point over to Michael. She needed to tell him in a way that he would understand. She knew he was a man of integrity and honor, but she also knew he felt her give in to his kiss. She felt him harden as she slid down his body. He knew she enjoyed the kiss just like he did or she would not have returned his kiss with such passion. So, how was she going to tell him that it couldn't happen again; ever? This was a nightmare she walked into with her eyes wide open and she wanted to wake up and it would be all over then things would be back like they were before the kiss. But she wasn't sleep. She was wide awake and she didn't know what to do.

She tossed and turned and couldn't get comfortable. Finally, out of frustration and anxiety, she got up and went to the kitchen to start dinner. Two minutes later, Michael walked into the kitchen looking as confused and concerned as she felt.

He looked at Mary and said, "Short nap?"

"Nope. No nap." she answered and they both laughed, knowing that neither one of them had slept.

He sat down at the far end of the island and his piercing eyes staring at her made her more nervous than she was already. She stopped and looked him directly in the eye. Mary knew that God had given her this perfect moment to do what had to be done. She silently prayed that she could say what had to be said. She also asked God to attune Michael's ears so that he would listen with his heart. She asked God to let their hearts be on the same page and not their heads; or rather not their bodies rule against what they knew in their hearts was the right thing to do. She wanted to use this perfect opportunity right now, but for some reason, she couldn't get her mouth to say anything.

Michael started talking in general about how things happen in strange ways at strange times. He was dancing all around what he really wanted to say and Mary knew exactly what that was, so she decided to just jump right in with both feet.

"Michael, I enjoyed our kiss." She said followed by a long pause.

"As a matter of fact, I will most likely never ever forget it" She paused again and took a long calming breath.

Michael looked puzzled and before she continued, he asked, "Why's that Mary? Why will you never ever forget our first kiss?"

"It's the kind of kiss that normally precedes other intimacies. It was the kind of kiss that leads to affirmations of love and life lived as one."

Michael took a deep breath, "I know."

She continued, "That's where the problem is. Between us, it can't go any further. Well, actually, it could go further if I permitted it to go further, but I can't do that. It has nothing to do with you as a man nor am I saying that I was not affected by it. The fact is, I have taken a vow of celibacy. I have pledged before God to remain sexually pure until I marry again."

She stopped for a breath and Michael's expression had not changed, so she continued, "You see Michael, I like you a lot, and I think you like me too. We enjoy each other's company and we have a lot of things in common and that is unusual. So it's only natural that we would normally take the relationship to the next level which is getting to know each other on a physical level. I am so sorry if I led you to believe that I was ready to take it to that next level, because, I really can't do it. I promise you that I'm not a flirt nor am I the kind of woman that's *easy*." she said, using her fingers to put the quotation marks around the word easy. She continued, "I am a normal red-blooded woman who enjoys what all adults enjoy. The difference is that I have chosen to wait for God to send another man into my life who will become my husband. Until then I will remain sexually inactive. This is not a decision that I made easily or hastily, but one made after much prayer and fasting. I have been celibate for 23 years." She stopped to catch her breath and added, "That's all I wanted to say."

She realized it came as a shock to Michael because this is the 21st century and sex is everywhere you look. She was sure that he never heard of a 60 year old mother of three grown children declare that she would not have sex until she married again? He got a glimpse of how uninhibited she was on that score, so he didn't have to wonder much what kind of sex partner she would be. She was a sexy, passionate woman. At least that's what her first husband used to tell her. She used to really, really push all his buttons! Naturally, he pushed all of hers too. But saying that for 23 years she had not had sex was probably hard to believe. She hoped he believed her even if it was hard to accept.

She wondered if he thought she was nuts. She felt like disappearing right then, but she had to hear what he had to say. She thanked God for giving her the strength and the words to tell him where she really stood, even after their hot and soulful kiss. Mary knew the words came from the Holy Spirit because she had no idea what to say. She was just glad she'd gotten them out. She silently thanked God for being there like He said He would.

She turned back to the counter and to pour the cornbread batter into the pan. She held her breath waiting for Michael to speak. It took him several minutes to get his thoughts together but when he did, she was absolutely shocked! She didn't know how to react to a man she hardly knew, who just happened to be a millionaire, who told her that he was falling in love with her, and that he would wait and let God show her that they belonged together. She knew what she was feeling about him, but she was totally unprepared to hear him openly confess his love for her. They had only met 26 hours ago.

She asked him to set the table and he slowly got up and came around to where she was standing and eased her onto a stool. He slowly bent down and softly said that he wanted to let her know that he would be kissing her again, but that he would tone it down and keep it on the right level. He said that was the best he could do. He told her to expect to be kissed more and more, as long as he was alive. He lifted her chin and very lightly planted the softest sweetest kiss on her lips. All she could do was lovingly look up at him, smile, and thank God for His mercy.

Michael set the table and soon they sat down to eat. Mary gave some consideration to everything that had happened between them. She hoped that because they had openly and honestly shared their feelings, everything would be even more relaxed between them, and she was right. They teased each other more and even played a few games of Scrabble after dinner.

Later that night, when it was finally time to go to bed, they did kiss each other good night, but it was nothing like the passionate kiss they had experienced in the same place in the hall earlier that day. For some reason, Mary was of the opinion that tomorrow would be another day full of surprises. She knew she would sleep better than she did last night. She figured Michael would too.

She talked to God; she told Him how awesome He is. She did believe just like Mama Lou said, that God made Michael just for her, and sent him to her because it was time for her to make some changes. "Thank you God. I think. Now PLEASE, help me to hold on and hold out until the time comes and we are united as one in Your presence."

MICHAEL

He probably should not have been surprised to find Mary in the kitchen this afternoon when he went to get a drink of water. She obviously couldn't sleep either. Anyway, on a normal day, neither one of them had the luxury of sleeping during the day. It was a crazy idea in the first place.

She was probably thinking about their kiss and regretting it. Michael definitely didn't regret it; not for one second. He knew that the exciting and passionate kiss caught both of them off guard; it had his imagination running wild; truly a kiss to remember forever. It was the kiss that told his heart what his head couldn't believe. Michael was falling in love with his angel, Mary Elizabeth Cross.

She did surprise him talking about the kiss. Even though she said she wasn't the kind of woman that the kiss might have suggested she was, she assured him that she was serious about her vow of celibacy. He could not believe it. He had finally begun thinking about his personal tomorrows. He started thinking about sharing his blessings with a woman, who he was sure, loved him and whom he loved. Then the very woman in his thoughts drops a 100 pound anvil on his head and has him reeling like a drunken man trying to walk on ice.

He listened to her and then he heard his voice say words that he didn't tell his lips to say. "Mary. My sweet angel; Mary Elizabeth. I know you are not a flirt and that you don't have any ulterior motives. I understand that your body is the temple where the Holy Spirit lives. I respect your intention to remain sexually inactive until you are married. What I want you to know is that I will be the man you marry. I am falling in love with you. I don't know when it happened but I can tell you right now it's a done deal. I cannot imagine living without you in my life. Yes, I am aware that we have only known each other a short time, but I know the way you make me feel. You make me feel whole. You are the kind of woman that I have never had but always hoped for; longed for; for whom I prayed. You are the kind of woman I always dreamed of marrying. You are the one God made for me. I am not asking you to do anything except give us a chance. Let's continue to get to know each other and allow God answer our prayers. He's the One who can give us what we both desire. In fact, I think he already did."

Mary said nothing and he wasn't sure she even understood what he just said. But the atmosphere around the table was relaxed and things felt right; they felt good. Michael was totally relaxed and had let his guard down. He trusted his angel with his heart. Somehow, he knew she wouldn't hurt him. How he knew, he wasn't sure, but in his heart, he just knew it. This was his woman, his angel, his Mary Elizabeth and she would be his wife one day, and it wouldn't be very long. When he stopped and thought about the reality of it all, he felt like he was in a dream, but his heart and the smile on is angel's face said it was very real.

Yesterday, when he woke up, he was the CEO of two multi-million dollar corporations living in the fast lane with a corporate jet, women in every major city who would come when he called and do anything he wanted. He had parties to attend and bank accounts full of his own money that was his to spend any way he wanted.

Now, twenty-four hours later, he was a sixty-two year old man falling in love with a beautiful sixty year old woman, who is a widow, the mother of three grown children and eight grandchildren, who had taken a vow of celibacy before God. She intends to remain celibate until she gets married. She didn't know who or even if she would ever get married, let alone that she was marrying Michael. Come to think of it, Michael didn't know he was getting married either until he heard his mouth say it! What a mind-blowing twenty-four hours! All because of a winter storm! He couldn't wait to see what the next twenty-four hours had in store.

The rest of the evening was a blur of cleaning up the kitchen, playing games, laughing, talking, teasing each other and being completely relaxed and unguarded. When they went down the hall to their bedrooms neither was sure what to expect.

Michael just knew that he needed to kiss her to reassure them both that they were ok. They slowed and eventually stopped when they got to their bedroom doors just like before. He opened his arms and Mary walked into them. They held each other for what seems like hours without talking, squeezing, touching or even moving; just feeling each other breathe was enough.

Finally, he lifted her chin and kissed her softly on the lips. She kissed the palm of his left hand and after touching it gently to her cheek, they said good night.

It was a beautiful start to the rest of their lives together, because they both knew that they had become a couple. They were inching closer to becoming a permanent couple; husband and wife, much to their surprise.

CHAPTER 3

Wednesday, November 19

MARY ELIZABETH

Mary woke up thanking God for the change that was taking place in her life. The prospect of having a soul mate excited her and she couldn't help but smile. Then her nose said "hello!" She smelled coffee and bacon. She hurried up and got changed and went to the kitchen to find her giant bent down looking into the refrigerator. "Can I help you find something", she asked.

He turned and said, "Good morning, beautiful. Where's the milk? I wanted to make you some pancakes, but I can't find any milk."

"Good morning yourself, good looking," she responded.

"We're out of milk except powdered or evaporated. Tell you what, you made the coffee and fried the bacon, so why don't I do the pancakes and eggs?"

"Deal!" he replied as he handed her a bowl.

She got their breakfast finished and Michael sat their plates on the kitchen island. Just then they heard a phone and they both remembered his cell phone in her car in the garage. Mary ran and got it and quickly gave it to him. The conversation was brief and he hung up. They gave thanks for their food and enjoyed a good breakfast and some amazing coffee. He wouldn't tell Mary the secret, but she believed it had some vanilla and cinnamon in it.

They cleaned the kitchen together and proceeded to discuss the day's plans. Later in the afternoon, Mary was taking her neighbor some canned veggies and invited Michael to accompany her. She knew Mama Lou wanted to meet this giant living in her house, and to be honest, Mary wanted to get her opinion of him. Later they planned to make calls to check on others they hadn't spoken with since the storm. For lunch, because Michael had fried too much bacon for breakfast, they had BLT sandwiches with tomato soup. For dinner, they were having baked chicken and garlic potatoes.

Mary called Pastor Caldwell to make sure she wasn't missing any activities at Shiloh. But just as she figured, everything was shut down. She spoke with the hospital and thankfully they only had two babies in the pediatric unit where she volunteered, so she wasn't needed. Everyone urged her to stay in and keep warm. The library, like the church bookstore was also closed. Mary hoped she could get to the nursing home for her Bible study class on Friday, because she knew how the ladies enjoyed their study. They'd be disappointed if it was cancelled.

Michael talked to someone about getting his car and picking him up. He told whomever he was speaking with that he wanted a call when things were arranged. He also cancelled several meetings to be rescheduled at a later date. It was obvious that the snow storm was really wreaking havoc on his schedule. He asked that reservations be made for dinner at Foxwoods for Saturday night. He wanted his jet ready to go to Chicago on Monday. He gave authorization to RSVP several holiday functions including the Red and White Ball. He asked to have a man named Phillip to give him a call as soon as possible. His last call was to his parents. He assured them that he was great and that he would see them as soon as he was able to get home.

The calls didn't take long for either of them. Mary was done first and then Michael finished his. That's when they realized there was nothing to do with the rest of their day. Just as the atmosphere began to get electrified, and full of heavy pauses, they headed in different directions. Mary headed to the garage, and Michael headed to his bedroom.

Mary heard someone tapping on the back door and she knew it was Mama Lou which immediately filled her with anxiety. How on earth did she get over here with all the snow and ice on the ground, Mary wondered? When she opened the door Mama Lou quickly moved around her and saw Michael standing in the hallway.

"Well it's about time I got to meet this giant of a man with the tiny red car. I'm Ruthie Louise Thompson and who might you be?" she said jokingly.

Michael came back into the kitchen with a big smile on his face and extended his hand as he answered, "Hello Ruthie Louise Thompson. I am Michael Scott."

For a moment they both stared at each other and then the light bulb went on at the same time for them. "Are you Mama Ruth who used to live in Montgomery County, Georgia? Did you work for Robert and Irene Scott?"

She made Michael back all the way into the living room with her cane where he fell into a chair. She leaned over him and took her glasses off and wiped them on her apron. She lifted his face up and squealed, "Lil' Mike with the dimpled chin! Oh my goodness. You're my Lil' Mike!"

All of a sudden Mike stood up and engulfed Mama Lou in his arms picking her up off the floor and swinging her around and around both of them laughing like school children.

"Boy, you put me down before you fall! Quit that now. I mean it! Listen here boy, have you lost your mind? Put me down right now! I mean it now Lil' Mike, put me down."

He gently set her down. They hugged and he released her and led her to the sofa. Needless to say, Mary was as shocked with their display of affection. They started to talk about Georgia and people they knew and things that happened back then and Mary left them to get reacquainted. Who knew that her Mama Lou was Michael's Mama Ruth? It's a small world!

Mary came back into the living room carrying a tray of hot water and teabags with lemon slices, sugar, honey, cream and teacakes. Mama Lou beamed with happiness and Michael looked so content.

Mary realized, while listening to their exchange of stories and antics, that Michael was her favorite of all the cousins who used to descend from the north to the south during the summer. She kept talking about Michael's height and how it skips generations and that he got it from some Scotts she knew when his dad and his brothers were little boys. They talked for hours and she enjoyed listening, hearing about Michael's growing up years. The more she heard, the more she knew that this was the man God had made specifically for her. She could feel her heart open more and more, like a rose bud gradually turning into a rose. She felt beautiful and loved as he glanced at her often and lovingly throughout the afternoon reunion.

Mama Lou's visit helped make the time pass rather quickly and before long Mary mentioned she needed to get dinner started. They invited Mama Lou to stay and after very little prodding, she agreed.

The evening was wonderful, listening to Mama Lou tell stories about the Scott boys and girls growing up. Mary didn't know Mama Lou could remember so much of the past, but they did know she could talk. It was a wonderful way to spend a cold Thursday evening.

Mama Lou announced that it was getting close to her bedtime, so they walked her home. While Michael was making her a fire and checking the house for leaks, Mama Lou took Mary by the hand and walked into her bedroom, "Listen to me real good now Mary Elizabeth. Lil' Mike is a good man because he was a good boy. You see all the good he does from reading the papers. He looks at you with love in his eyes. I know what that look means because I've seen it before. Don't let this man slip away from you. You deserve some happiness and he's the one who can give it to you."

Mary wasn't shocked by what she said, but she was touched by the sincerity of her words.

"I know Mama Lou. He has told me so himself." She paused and then slowly added, "And I love him too. We don't know what's going to happen next, but we're letting God guide the relationship."

Mama Lou opened her arms and Mary went to her. They hugged and kissed each other's cheeks. When they separated, Mama Lou wiped the tears from her face and Mary's too.

Just then Michael called out, "Okay, ladies, it's impolite to leave company all alone." Mary hugged and kissed Mama Lou while Michael waited his turn. He bent low and picked Mama Lou up and kissed her, put her down and then reached for Mary's hand as they left the house. Michael turned back to Mama Lou and said very gently, "Mama, if you need anything, just call. Don't you come outside unless one of us is with you, okay?"

Mama Lou smiled and said, "Okay, Lil' Big Mike."

Michael

What an amazing day! Michael could hardly believe that his childhood Mama Ruth is still alive and in such good health. She remembered things that even he had forgotten. He would have to let his cousins know he'd found their Mama Ruth. He knew they would be just as excited to hear the news.

The temperature was getting warmer and the snow and ice was starting to melt. Very soon he would have to get back to the life he had before Monday afternoon. There was only one thing wrong. He really didn't want to go back to the life he had before Monday afternoon. What would make him happy would be to spend the rest of his days and nights with Mary Elizabeth. Just thinking about going back to the corporate jungle of deals, crisis prevention and intervention management made him sad. He had to look forward to flying from one city to another, living in nameless hotels and attending meetings with snipers sitting around the table waiting for an opportunity to strike. Michael thought about how his life would be different if he could come home every evening to the love and warmth of his angel Mary Elizabeth, this woman he loved. Or how the endless meetings across the country and abroad would be so much better if Mary Elizabeth was with him and he could come home to her wherever he was. Those were happy thoughts and they made him smile.

As he prepared for bed, Michael thanked God for keeping his Mama Ruth safe and in good health all these 40 years since he had last seen her. He asked God to continue to keep Mama Ruth safe and to show him what he could do to make her life better.

Then he had to thank God again for the blessing of meeting his soul mate. His prayer was that somehow, he desperately wanted to keep her in his life. He knew she didn't believe she could deal with his world, but he was sure that she could handle it like a pro. He thought, 'She will take to it like a duck to water'. He just had to show her more of his world and gradually introduce her to his family and associates. He didn't really have any close friends, only Leon and Phillip. He wanted to assure her that he would always be near and he dared a living soul to give her one moment of anxiety. He had a plan and it would begin Friday, as soon as he could meet with Phillip. This holiday will be one he knew he would never forget. Hopefully, his angel would see his love and open her heart and embrace it. He had no doubt that she could easily navigate through his world. He began trying to decide between emeralds, rubies or all diamonds for her engagement ring. Green represented growth and new life. He settled on diamonds and emeralds. "Perfect!" he said, his last thought before falling into another night of restful, deep, peaceful sleep. He was feeling her hands on him, and smelling her soft scent. Torture for sure, but oh, such sweet torture.

CHAPTER 4

Thursday, November 20

The beautiful white snow continued to melt making puddles of muddy water and slush. Things would be back to normal very soon. Michael shoveled the sidewalks and driveway at Mama Lou's and Mary's house. He was finally able move his car which he parked in Mary's driveway.

He wasn't very talkative and neither of them wanted anything more than coffee and toast for breakfast. She still couldn't go to the church to work in the bookstore because the church was still closed. She rearranged her linen closet and packed away some winter clothes for the church's clothes pantry. Michael spent most of his time outside doing things at Mama Lou's.

He stopped for lunch and had a bowl of creamy potato soup, spinach salad with tomatoes and eggs, and some melt in your mouth bread pudding. When he finally got back to Mary's it was almost dark. He went to his room and remained there for almost 2 hours.

Mary didn't bother to call him to dinner, because she knew he could smell the food. She had gone out of her way to make it a special meal, since it was bound to be their last one for some time. Mary had showered and changed her clothes and set the table with candles and wine glasses and her best china. She thought maybe Michael was feeling the same as she was and just didn't want to face it. The fact was that their time together was ending tomorrow.

She checked the food again to make sure everything was okay. The bread was in the warmer, the roast was in the oven, the veggies were in the chafing dish, the wine was chilling and the dessert was waiting to be served. The only thing needed was Michael.

Mary debated with herself whether to knock on his door or just wait. She tried to convince herself that he might have some sore muscles from shoveling and lifting all the heavy snow and ice. He had also cleaned all snow and ice from his car. But somehow, Mary knew that nothing was wrong with him, except dreading the inevitable. Staying in his room was not going to slow the clock.

Just as she was about to check on him, he came out of the room. He looked so good. He had on his slacks and white shirt opened at the collar. His mustache was trimmed and it looked like he had even polished his shoes. He was the most handsome man Mary had ever seen. She didn't realize she was holding her breath until he smiled at her and she finally took a breath.

Mary felt less self-conscious about herself after seeing that he, too, had spent a little extra time preparing for their last dinner. She had put on a long sleeve gray jersey dress that fit her waist and from a thin red patent leather belt, the dress flared down just below her knees. She wore red patent pumps and a beautiful red brooch and matching earrings. The whole ensemble was quite stylish and she looked elegant yet understated, gorgeous yet natural. She was so beautiful. She was like a whisper instead of a scream. Michael had to hold himself in check lest he grab her and take their night in a direction he knew she would not welcome.

They ate in an atmosphere that was pregnant with unspoken emotions. Soft jazz played from the den which infused the mealtime with that little touch of something special. The conversation was minimal and yet You could feel the love that was in the air. It was evident when they looked at each other, the smiles and the blush that came to Mary's cheeks every now and then.

When Mary went to get the dessert, Michael cleared the table. He offered to carry the dessert tray; Mary gave it to him and got the coffee. When they set everything on the table, Michael looked at Mary and she stopped in her tracks. He took one step and stopped as Mary's heart slowed and she knew what was coming. Michael held out his hand and she walked up to him and took it. He raised her hand to his lips and kissed it gently. He lifted her face up and when they were looking into each other's eyes he tilted his head ever so slightly and kissed her palm. Time stood still.

Michael bent down and kissed Mary's upturned lips. She kissed him back and he pulled her body to him and she filled the space like she had done it for years. They kissed for what seemed like an eternity and when their lips separated, they both moaned. They continued to hold each other in silence, as no words were necessary. Ever so slowly Mary moved to her chair and Michael pulled it out for her and kissed the top of her head. When he sat, he took her hands in his and stared deeply into her eyes. All he saw was love and the life he never dreamed he would ever have.

"Mary, meeting you and spending these few days with you has impacted my life like nothing else has ever done. I love you without a doubt and yet I can't tell you how that happened. I just know that I do and I won't deny it and I won't try to explain it. I believe God brought us together for a reason. I hope it was so that we could meet our soul mate that He designed for us before we were even born.

"My life is absolutely complete with you in it. I cannot imagine living without you in my life. I hope you feel the same way. I want you to be my wife. I want to share my life with you and I want to be a part of your life."

He paused and waited for her response. She looked down, and then back up into his eyes. She indeed saw all the love a woman could ask for from a man. She knew Michael was her soul mate. She would not and could not deny her love for him, but she hesitated before speaking which worried Michael.

"Michael, this has been the most incredible few days of my life. I have felt things with you that I never thought would be possible. I can feel your love for me. My heart is so full with love for you that sometimes when I get near you, I think my heart just might burst because it is so full of joy. I have no doubt that you would care for me if I was a part of your life. My concern is not your love, but your world. I don't know whether I can fit into your world or your lifestyle, Michael. You are constantly on the go, and you move in circles that I'm not sure would be comfortable for me. I know the social graces and how to carry myself, but I don't know if I would be enough for you. I have things that I love to do and would not like to stop doing them just because I was the wife of a millionaire. Do you understand what I'm saying, Michael?"

"Angel, you are absolutely all I need. If there is anything that you might not be comfortable doing or not understand, I will help you, teach you, and do whatever needs to be done to make you comfortable. I would not expect you to change anything about your life for me. What you do makes you who you are and I love who you are. I just need us to be together. All

I want is to spend the rest of my life loving you and laughing with you or eating with you and kissing you or making love to you and seeing the world with you.

"I want to start my day looking into your eyes and saying, 'Good morning angel', praying together, eating breakfast together and sharing our daily plans with each other. I want to end each day with you doing the same thing. I will never be whole again without you, because you, Mary Elizabeth, are the other half of me. Without you, my life will be incomplete. I can't be all that I can be without you in my life, helping me be an even better me and supporting my dreams just as I will support yours."

"The words sound beautiful Michael and I know you are sincere. I really can't deny that I don't want to face the rest of my life without you either. But we will have to go slow. Can you promise me we'll go slowly at first?"

Michael knelt in front of Mary and said, "Mary Elizabeth Cross, I love you more than anything or anyone in this world. Would you do me the honor becoming my wife?"

Mary took his face in her hands and as tears slid down her face, she said with a smile, "Yes, Michael David Scott, I will marry you."

Michael asked "When?" She laughed and kissed his forehead, "sooner than later, that's for sure."

He laughed and asked about February, Valentine's Day? Mary still smiling said, "Wow, that's right around the corner. You call that slowly? Why don't we say June? That way, I will have time to gather my family so they can meet you and plan the wedding; which I get the feeling is quickly going to become the talk of Hartford and a lot bigger than I want? If we wait until June, we can be sure there will be no snow to contend with."

Michael frowned and rubbed his head, "June is a long way away. That's 193 days of waiting! But, if you, Mary Elizabeth want June 3, then June 3 it will be. Well, I guess I'd better get off my knees and get my iPad and get you a paper and pen so we can start setting some guidelines."

Mary repeated, "Guidelines?"

Michael stood and started pacing, "Yes, absolutely!" He stopped and turned and looked at her with the biggest grin on his face and ticked off on his fingers, "No dancing down the aisle; no lilac cummerbunds; no fuchsia bow ties; and for sure no white shoes!" They both laughed. Mary jumped up from the table and went into his arms where he hugged and kissed her as if he would never end it. When they parted, they moved into the living room and with paper and pen, iPad and their feet on the coffee table, they began tackling their wedding plans which were off to a fun start.

They spent hours discussing their ideas for their wedding and Mary did her best to keep things modest while Michael kept wanting to take everything over the top. Nothing was settled, but it looked like they had agreed on June 3 as the date. They also agreed on a small to medium sized affair. Mary kept thinking it was getting bigger the more Michael talked. They had also decided to marry in a church, but couldn't pinpoint which one. The reception would be at the Foxwoods or the Convention Center. Everything else was still to be worked out. Michael gave her carte blanche. He knew it would be beautiful. He also knew she would not spend nearly as much as he would if she let him take care of everything. At about 2:35am they finally put their plans to bed and decided to retire for the night.

CHAPTER 5

Friday Morning, November 21

The world would be perfect if only Michael and Mary could hold on to the loving feelings they had right now. But, as it is with everything else in life, the clock continues to tick, and tomorrow brings reality back into focus, like it or not. People make plans while life has a way of altering those plans.

In the early morning hours, without saying a word, they slowly made their way down the hall, probably for the last time for many months. They got to the bedrooms and turned into each other's arms, both thinking how it would be so easy to end their day making love to each other. Both were thinking of ways they would like to pleasure the other. Finally, still without so much as a whisper, Michael kissed her on top of her head and when she looked up, saw unshed tears in his eyes. She softly touched his cheek and stood on her tiptoes to kiss his lips. She entered her room and faced the future waiting to be Michael's wife. She put her fist to her mouth to keep the moan from coming out as she fell onto her bed and cried for the first time in a very long time.

Michael wiped the tears that were now flowing freely down his face. He had never been so happy and so miserable at the same time. He sat and slowly took off his shoes and socks. He hung up his pants and shirt while thinking about all the things he wanted to do with Mary. Places he wanted to take her, things he wanted to give her and ways he wanted to make love to her. He sighed and fell into his bed staring at the ceiling. Could he really wait until June to make love to his angel? He knew in his heart that he could wait and he knew in his head that he would have to, but he wasn't sure how to do it. Would the plans he was making please Mary? He wasn't sure. The only thing he knew for sure was the he was in love for the first time in his life. Really in love and he wanted to show his woman and the whole world how much she meant to him. He was going for broke and hoped she would understand his motives. He was pulling out all the stops and the sky was the limit for his future and his bride to be.

He thought about his parents. He hoped, they too, would understand his motives and be as pleased with his plans as he was. He had no doubt that they would love Mary Elizabeth because you couldn't know her and not love her. He also knew they would know how much he loved her and most importantly, why he loved her.

They would be so excited to know he had found Mama Ruth. He finally drifted off to sleep thinking about what a joyful reunion they would all have when his family came for the wedding and could see their Mama Ruth after all these years.

Mary Elizabeth crept into Michael's room just as he was drifting off to sleep and slipped into his bed. He thought he was dreaming until he felt her soft hair touching his chin and smelled the light scent of vanilla and honey in his nose. She snuggled up to him with her softness up against his rapidly rising manhood. He wanted to roll her onto her back and claim her as his for all time. Instead, he wrapped his arm around her and held her. Sleep descended upon them like a sweet fragrant cocoon, slowly and without a word. They drifted off dreaming of multi- tiered wedding cakes and flowers; doves; butterflies; laughter; family; friends and tears of joy. He held her close saying nothing and Mary was grateful. No words were needed. Words could not change the situation nor could it speed up the clock to their future. They simply had to live life and wait.

Michael woke with a smile on his face not moving for fear of disturbing Mary whose breathing was slow and rhythmic. He wanted to wake her but he did not look forward to what this day meant.

She finally moved and turned to face him, startled to see his eyes open, looking at her. He was still smiling when he said, "Morning, beautiful." She smiled and said, "Good morning to you, good looking." They kissed and hugged each other. Mary noticed his erection nestled close to her and she shuttered. He eased back and she scooted up so she could lean on her elbow. She smiled and patted his face as she started to get out of bed. "Soon, I'll be able to help you with your morning stiffness. I know how it is for you senior citizens when you first get up. Your old bones have a mind of their own sometimes and just won't cooperate, will they?" She winked and scooted out of bed just out of reach before he grabbed her. He swore under his breath and wondered, briefly, what he would have done had he caught her. He reclined back against the headboard and said, "I'm going to remember your little smart remark, Mary Elizabeth Cross. You're pay for making fun of my little dilemma. That's number one."

He wanted to stay in her bed and in her house forever, but duty called, and he had lots of responsibilities and duties that awaited him. People were depending on him and he had a lot of new things to add to his already busy plate.

He showered and dressed slowly, thinking about the fact that Mary had come to him last night. She had actually gotten in bed with him and slept there all night. He knew what it meant to him. He felt like it meant that she loved and trusted him to keep his word. He had done that and he had not lost any respect for her. He knew that it was her way of giving them both as much closeness as she could without going over the line or taking a chance on breaking her vow. He took a piece of his personalized note paper from his briefcase and wrote her a note about last night. He wanted to help reduce any stress she may be feeling about it; and he wanted to make her smile. He put the note on the pillow, knowing that she would find it when she changed the linen. That thought made him smile. Knowing Mary, she would probably change the linen today.

He got his briefcase and lap top and headed out the door. He looked around one last time, taking a photo of the room storing it in the photo album in his mind. He would never forget it and the peace, joy, and love he found while he slept here. The peaceful spirit in this house would always be with him. He knew that when they married, Mary would fill his house with loving warmth and joy just like this house. She made all the difference and he looked forward to living in his house that would finally become their home.

Mary prayed that Michael would not take her coming into his bed last night the wrong way. Her desire to be near him was so strong that she imagined she could hear him calling her. When she had no more tears to cry, she showered and lay across her bed hearing her heart speak and wondering whether she should give in. At last, she got up, went into his bedroom and got in bed with him. She knew he wasn't quite sleep, but he didn't make things hard for her by speaking or acknowledging her presence. That fact alone spoke volumes to her heart. When he put his arm around her, she knew he understood. However, now, in the light of day, she wasn't so sure. She decided if he didn't bring it up, she wouldn't either. She dressed quickly in black corduroy pants, a pink and white blouse with a black sweater.

They emerged from their rooms at the same time. They reached for each other's hand and went down the hall to face the world as a couple in love. Only time would tell what the world would throw at them, but they knew without a doubt, that together, they'd face it. They had God on their side and the victory was already theirs.

He put his things in the living room and went into the kitchen to help with breakfast. And what a breakfast it was! It was more like a morning buffet-feast with omelets, biscuits; bacon; eggs; grits; juice, and coffee. The food was delicious as always but it tasted even better than before. She had somehow given him different treats to remember, when he returned to his office, on those mornings when he'd be eating a cold Danish and drinking non-descript coffee. They talked a little trying to make plans for the weekend but only settled on having dinner Saturday evening.

Shortly after breakfast, Michael's car was towed away and his car service was out front waiting to take him away from her. He wanted to help clean the breakfast dishes, but she insisted that he get to his office. They both knew all kinds of chaos could be brewing since the office had been closed three days.

Finally, after much persuasion, he put on his coat and reached for Mary. She willingly went into his arms and he hungrily kissed her lips and nuzzled her neck. When he saw the tears in her eyes, he held her even closer while rubbing her back and reassured her that everything would be fine. He reminded her that he was in her life for the long haul.

He handed her a business card, "Here are all my numbers. They're on the night stand in my room too, just in case. Call me any time. I'm picking you up for dinner tomorrow night at seven. See you then, if not sooner. I love you, my angel. You're here forever, safe and secure," he said, pointing to his heart. "And don't ever forget I love you, Mary Elizabeth Cross."

She reached up and touched his face, rubbing her thumb across his lips. "I love you too, Michael. Please be careful and take care of yourself for me, my handsome giant. Remember I have someone here, she said patting to her heart, whom I love more than words can express. I'll see you soon my love."

He kissed her one last time before putting on his hat and opening the door to leave. Half way down the sidewalk, he turned, waved and said, "I love you, angel."

She stood in the door watching his driver open the car door for him and take his briefcase while he got in the car. After he was settled in the seat, the driver handed his briefcase back and shut the door. When the car pulled off, she heard Mama Lou behind her. She didn't turn around immediately, trying to give her tears time to dry up so Mama Lou wouldn't see her wipe them away. Quietly, Mama Lou came up beside her and gently put some tissue in her hand. Neither woman said a word, nor did they move from the door. Mary was grateful for Mama Lou's silence. She could think of nothing to say that would ease the emptiness she felt at that moment. She could not even begin to express in words what had just happened in her life over the past four days.

CHAPTER 6

Saturday, November 22

Saturday morning, Mary was awakened by someone knocking on her front door and hearing Mama Lou calling out to her from somewhere inside the house. She grabbed her robe and rushed down the hall where Mama Lou was opening the door for a delivery of some kind. The delivery man sat several boxes down in the living room and then he went back to the truck and got more boxes.

After he left, the women looked at each other and a slow smile formed on their faces. Each was a Neiman Marcus box and each box was labeled with one of their names. They knew without even saying a word that the boxes had come from Michael.

"Mama Lou, you go first." Mary said as she went to get scissors. She was far too nervous at the moment to open hers.

She piled Mama Lou's boxes on the sofa next to her and she selected her biggest box to open first. Mary helped her with the box and when they got it opened, Mama's hands flew to her mouth and she said in a whisper, "Oh Lord Jesus, what did my Lil' Mike do?"

She took out the most beautiful mahogany mink jacket with baby lamb trim and held it up in front of her. It was stunning. She rubbed on the fur and held it up to her face. "Put it on for me Mary, so I can see how it looks." When Mary put on the jacket and turned around for Mama Ruth to see, she just shook her head with tears streaming down her face. "I always talked about wearing a mink coat someday. I used to tell the children that when I got my money all saved up, it was going to be the first thing I bought for myself. My Lil' Mike remembered. He was really listening to me. What an absolutely beautiful mink jacket! This is really unbelievable", she said as she shook her head and wiped her nose.

"But this is the kind of man my Lil' Mike is, Mary. He's thoughtful, generous, and loving. I told you he was a good man."

The next box she opened held a beautiful teal tea-length evening dress. The dress had sheer three-quarter length sleeves with a cowl neck fitted bodice with a full skirt, accentuated with a matching satin sash with rhinestones on the bow. The next box contained silver shoes and a matching bag. The last box contained gloves and rhinestone jewelry. Mama Lou kept saying, "This is too much. This is just too much!" She'd pick up one thing and then another. Mary put the jacket around Mama's shoulders. She stood up and walked around like she was on the red carpet in Hollywood. When she sat back down, they both laughed and that's when she saw an envelope in the bottom of the last box. It was a hand-written note on Michael's personalized paper.

She read it aloud, "Sweet Mama Ruth, you are my special lady. Will you be my guest at dinner tonight? I tried to have an answer for every argument you could come up with so you couldn't say no to my invitation. If you don't like the gifts I selected, call this number and a shopper is available to help you with another selection at home or in the store. If you decide to go into the store, they will pick you up, so you won't have to worry about bothering Mary, even though you know it wouldn't be a bother. There is money in your bag for you to get all the other things you will say you need in order to be 'presentable' and 'properly dolled up' this evening. I love you Mama Ruth. You could go out to dinner with me just like you are right now. But I know you and that would never do. I know you will feel more comfortable if you have something new to wear tonight. So, please, make me happy and share this special evening with us. We love you dearly, Lil' Mike."

"Oh Mary, isn't he a wonderful man. I am so excited. Come on girl, open your boxes."

Mary began by opening a smaller box. It contained an evening bag, matching shoes, and gloves. She looked inside one of the shoes; and she thought, "Gosh, they are my size, too."

In the next box was a beautiful faux-wrap charcoal chiffon dress. She got up and held the dress against her. It was the most beautiful dress she had ever seen. The dress was sleeveless and had a low cut neckline with a rhinestone accent on the side.

The next box contained a lovely black one shoulder sequined gown that was fitted with a front split. Michael had excellent taste.

The next box contained a red lace fitted dress covered in pearls and sequins with long sheer sleeves, a short train and a standup satin collar. It looked like a dress a queen or a movie star would wear. It was magnificent!

The next box contained a hot pink gown that was ruche off the shoulder with an asymmetrical fish tail made with rows of tulle and satin. Her breath caught as she took it out of the box. She was overcome with emotions. The dresses were unbelievably beautiful.

They decided to try everything on and started gathering the things when the doorbell rang. Mary wondered what now as she went to the door. When she opened it, to her surprise it was the delivery man again. He apologized and said he had overlooked two boxes. Mary took them and when she tried to give him a tip, he said it was taken care of. She thanked him and shut the door wondering aloud, "What on earth could this be?"

The small box contained an invitation which read, "Mary Elizabeth Cross. I love you. I want you to wear whichever gown you want tonight. They were too pretty to pick just one, so I decided to buy them all. You'll have lots of events to wear them to during this holiday season. This is money for you to get all the other things that you think go along with an evening out to dinner with me. No, you won't have to do this every time we go out to dinner. Tonight is special. If you want to, you can make a standing appointment with your stylist and nail tech and they can come to your house and do whatever you want done any time, not just when we are going somewhere special. I have to run. I love you and I can't wait to see you tonight. I have written down what I think you'll wear, but I won't show you until after we get home. Forever loving you, Michael."

Mary smiled and looked up at Mama Ruth who was wiping her eyes and nose again. She reminded Mary that she had not opened the other box, so she did.

Mary's breath caught in her throat when she saw an extraordinarily beautiful full length black mink coat with silver fox trim. Mary had to sit down to compose herself. "Oh, my Gosh!" Mama Lou said. Mary was absolutely speechless.

Finally, Mama Lou said, "Alright, it's getting close to eight and we have to try on our stuff. Let's go child! We can't sit around all day. We have lots to do and only eleven hours so move it!" Mary got up and went to get her day started while Mama Ruth went into one of the other bedrooms to try on her stuff.

Mary called the hair salon for Mama Lou and asked if she could have the nail tech there when they arrived. The owner said she would take care of it. Mary requested a hair trim and edge-up for herself.

After a quick breakfast and getting dressed, they made it to the salon by eight forty-five. They finished a little before noon. Each had gotten manicures, pedicures, and facials. Mary had her hair trimmed, Mama Lou had hers relaxed, cut and styled. She looked like she was 20 years younger. She looked really good. Based on how she was acting, Mary could see that she felt good too. She kept reminding Mary of what they had to do next. She was like a drill sergeant with a fresh recruit. Maybe not barking orders, but certainly keeping up with the time and the tasks at hand. She was focused, excited and for sure intending to be ready whenever Michael came to pick her up tonight whether Mary was ready or not.

They bought new under garments and hosiery. Mary decided to splurge and get a new outfit for Sunday. She saw two that she liked so she did something she had never done for herself; she bought them both. She talked Mama Lou into buying herself a new Sunday hat and a new suit too. She had Mary drive her to a medical equipment store and she splurged and got herself a new 'proper' cane, as she called it. She was going to be stepping high and she intended for everything to be beautiful, new and proper.

As these two women headed back home, exhausted but happy, they were excited and eager as any two school girls getting ready for the prom. After a light lunch, Mama Lou went home to take a nap.

Mary tried to sleep too, but she was too excited. So, after tossing and turning for a while, she got up and decided to indulge in a bubble bath, something she hadn't done in many years. She was always on the go and over the years made herself satisfied with taking long steamy showers. But tonight was such a special occasion; it just seemed to call for a long luxurious bubble bath. She stayed in the tub for so long she began to wrinkle like a prune. She patted herself dry, moisturized her skin and lavishly applied lotion and skin cream. It was almost 5 o'clock so she started to apply her makeup. She knew how to do it, but it had been so long since she really made up her face. She had to be very careful and take her time because applying it in a hurry could and probably would be disastrous.

Finally, after putting on the finishing touch of some lightly tinted lip gloss, she went to the closet to select her gown. Mary had no idea who would be joining them at dinner tonight. She had a funny feeling that Michael's parents would be there for sure. Also joining them would probably be Phillip, his assistant that he talks about quite a bit. Of course, either of the dresses would look great because they all were perfect fits. After thinking about the impression each dress would make, she selected the hot pink one with the off the shoulder bodice and the fish tail bottom. It was not as revealing as some of the others. She figured they would come in handy when she had to be in the presence of some of his former lovers, lady friends, and colleagues. She didn't expect any of them to ever confront her, but she did intend to carry herself in a way that left no room for doubt as to who had all of Michael's love and attention.

The dress was laid out on the bed. So, dressed in undergarments and robe, Mary went into the kitchen to make a cup of tea. Just then Mama Lou tapped on the door and let herself in.

Mary looked up and saw a little brown, white-haired doll in a lovely teal gown with a gorgeous mink jacket. She had the biggest smile on her face. She had powdered her face and added a touch of red lipstick, which Mary had never seen her wear before! Mary ran and got her cell phone and without saying anything took her picture. Mama Lou jokingly scolded her, but she liked the picture, so Mary gave her time to get composed and do some really cute poses and took a few more pictures.

When she finished she asked Mary, "Child, why aren't you dressed yet? It's almost time to go." Actually, it was only 6:25. Mary told her, she was taking her tea back to the room so she could put on her dress and she'd be ready. She made herself a cup of tea and went to her room.

Fifteen minutes later, she stepped out of the room and her giant was standing at the end of the hall looking at her. He had the biggest smile on his face. His eyes were shining like he was about to cry. She smiled and he met her in the hall in about two seconds. She went into his arms and neither of them said a word. She could feel his heart beat and she knew he felt hers. Their hearts were beating to the same beat just like before.

He slowly held her away from him and said, "Damn baby, you were already beautiful. Now you are absolutely stunning! How can you be more than beautiful? I need another word for beautiful. Help me, Lord, give me a word to describe my angel."

He let out a soft moan and said softly, "Oh, Lord help me please. Mary, you make me want to do things to you."

Just then Mama Lou cleared her throat and said, "Okay you two, that's far enough. I have ears and eyes too. Let's get this party started."

Michael went to get their coats out of the closet. Mary came into the living room and Mama Lou whispered to her, "That's the perfect dress for tonight. Either of the others and I would have been forced to handcuff the giant's hands behind his back all night." Mary laughed and winked at his smiling face beaming like a spotlight.

Michael helped them into their coats. The three of them floated outside into the brisk early evening air. They left the house in a limo that was taking them into the future on a night that was going to change Mary's life forever. A night she would never forget.

They arrived at Foxwoods and after being assisted from the limo, each woman took their giant's arm and literally floated into one of the most upscale restaurants in Hartford. It was known for its views, its intimate atmosphere, delicious meals prepared by award winning chefs, and impeccable service.

After Michael assisted them with their coats, he turned to Mary, smiled and kissed her square in the mouth. She was stunned to say the least. Just as she was about to protest, Mama Lou asked, "Did you forget your other date Mike?" Michael chuckled and bent and kissed her on both cheeks.

They were still smiling when this strikingly handsome couple approached along with an unescorted gentleman. The man with the beautiful woman by his side looked like an older version of Michael. Michael kissed his mother and hugged his dad. The other gentleman smiled, nodded and did double thumbs up after shaking Michael's hand. Mary was introduced to the renowned Maurice "Jackson" Scott and his beautiful wife Dorothy Anderson Scott. The solitary gentleman was Phillip Austin. Mr. and Mrs. Scott hugged and kissed Mama Lou and they all had tears in their eyes. After almost 55 years, they were overjoyed to see her and know that she was well and living right here in Hartford.

They were ushered to their table, which was large and round. Everyone got comfortably seated; Mary sat on Michael's left, next to Mama, who sat next to Mrs. Scott. Mr. Scott sat by his wife, Phillip sat between him and Michael.

Following their drink orders being taken, Michael's father asked Mary how long she had been living in Hartford. When she told him a little over 30 years, he seemed stunned. She told him that after her husband retired from the military, the family moved there from Ft. Dix, New Jersey. She realized as soon as she said it that it would have a very shocking effect on everyone. It appeared, much to her surprise that only one person was affected; Mr. Scott.

The conversation was steered to more general topics and everyone seemed to be having a good time, except for Mr. Scott. Michael and Mary held hands as often as they could under the table. He would squeeze her hand when things got a little uncomfortable; like questions about Mary's husband's death. They made it through dinner and dessert. Mary opted not to have dessert, but Michael fed her part of his New York cheese cake. Mary thought Michael's dad was going to have a heart attack when Michael kissed her on the cheek. His mother just smiled.

After coffee Michael and Mary danced. Although the dance floor was rather small, they didn't see anyone in the room except each other. Much too soon, his father came out on the dance floor and asked Michael if he could cut in.

He and Mary danced in total silence for several minutes. Mary pondered what to say to this man who obviously did not care for her as his son's companion for the evening.

She prayed and asked God to give her the words to say so she could break through to this man's heart. She knew he loved his son and Michael adored his Dad. She needed to let him know who she was and what she was all about so he could relax. She didn't want their relationship to start off on the wrong foot.

Mary said to him," Mr. Scott, you don't like me very much do you?"

He was shocked that she would be so blunt, but he kept his composure and looked down at her, "Why do you say that Mrs. Cross? I have been cordial to you all evening."

"Yes you have, like a man handling a poisonous snake with a five foot pole. Mr. Scott, let me tell you something that you may have not considered while you are forming your opinion about Michael and I being together. First, neither one of us was looking for a life partner, so we were not expecting to meet someone as completely matched as we are; like opposite sides of the same coin.

"Second, when you live as long as Michael and I, you definitely know the type of person you would like to spend time with. I expect Michael desires my company because I am exactly the kind of person he has been waiting for.

"Third, I am not in love with Michael for what he has or for what he could do for me or give me. I am only interested in your son for one reason. He is the one man who makes my heart sing whenever I'm in his presence; the man who lights up my world when he says, "Good morning, beautiful.""

"I don't know anything about his world, and frankly, I feel like a fish out of water just thinking about it. The idea of having to be in the circles with people who make more money in a week than I make in a year terrifies me. But you know what, Mr. Scott? Michael wants me in that world with him, by his side, and with God's blessings that is exactly where I'll be. I love your son and he loves me. We can't help how we feel nor can we change it. "I just wanted to ease your mind and let you know that Michael's happiness is my only concern; not his money, his prestige or his name. I simply love the man, sir…just Michael …the man. That's all I wanted to say."

Mr. Scott held Mary away from him and he was about to say something when Michael came up and said, "Sorry, dad, but your time is up. I missed you angel." He kissed Mary on the lips and his dad just stared, turned and left the dance floor with a strange look on his face.

When they returned to the table, Mama Lou and Mrs. Scott had gone to the ladies lounge so Mary excused herself and joined them. Mama Lou was holding court in the lounge and talking to the women in front of the mirrors.

Mary sat on the sofa and turned to speak to Mrs. Scott when Mrs. Scott said, "Mary, you are a stunning beauty and I know that my son loves you. He loves the woman you are, not just your outer beauty. Not only that, you can hold your own with people by speaking your mind; and believe me you will need that in the circles he travels in. I saw you on the dance floor telling Jack a thing or two. Let me tell you something. He was blown away by whatever you said. He's used to leaving others speechless, but you got him real good. Thank you for speaking your mind, and doing it in such a classy way."

Mama added her amen and they all high fived. Mary went to the mirror to fix her lipstick. Mrs. Scott came up and stood beside Mary and softly said, "Mary, since we are going to be mother and daughter, do you think you could call me Dorothy or Mom or something other than Mrs. Scott? That sounds so formal, as if we don't like each other and which most definitely is not and will not be true."

Mary was utterly humbled and touched by this gesture of kindness being offered to her by her almost mother-in-law. She had no idea when

Michael had told his parents that he wanted to marry her, but obviously they knew.

Mary said, "You're right of course. How does Mama Dot sound?" Mrs. Scott smiled and said, "Mama Dot. I like it; it sounds snazzy- like you." They hugged and Mama Dot and Mama Lou left to rejoin the others. Michael's mother was down to earth and a very gracious woman. Mary liked her and knew she would enjoy being in her company.

Mary came out shortly after them. She was stopped in the hall by Mr. Scott and she braced herself for a tirade she was sure was coming her way. Instead, he took her arm and steered her to an area with a settee. He asked her to sit with him a moment and she did. He seemed to be having trouble forming his words, but she waited without saying anything. Then he cleared his throat and began.

"Michael is my only son and I suppose you could say I'm a little overprotective of him. I know he's a grown man, but he's still my son and I love him very much. Like you, his happiness means the world to me. The people that we normally associate with are all very status conscious and eager to move up the social ladder. Some of the women Michael has dated in the past have openly propositioned him, thinking that if they could get him, then his fortune will be theirs as well. I taught him long time ago to be cautious when it came to his heart because once the heart is broken it takes a long time to heal.

"I didn't want him to live his life without the love of a good woman who truly loved him; I just wanted him to be sure. When I look at the way you look at each other, the little whispers; the smiles; the kisses; and the chemistry, I would be blind not to see the love you share for each other. It almost sizzles whenever you touch each other."

He paused, and then continued, "I can relax now. I know after watching you and then after listening to you, I know his heart is safe. It's in the hands of the only woman who has ever given herself to him completely and who wanted him just for himself, not for what he had or what he could do for them. I thank you for loving my son, Mrs. Scott. I will be proud to have you in my family."

He leaned over and kissed her cheek, stood, offered his arm and she took it. Just before they took a step, he handed her his handkerchief and Mary dried my eyes, wiped her nose and handed it back to him. He said, "Mary, I don't want you to call me Mr. Scott. Sounds so old and stuffy. How about calling me Papa or Dad?"

Mary smiled and said, "How about Papa Jack?" He replied, "Sounds perfect; just perfect."

Smiling at each other when they entered the ballroom, his wife and Mama Lou saw the change in them, but Michael and Phillip were in the middle of a conversation so he only glanced at Mary as he touched her hand. Mrs. Scott and Mama Lou noticed the subtle change. They both smiled and Mrs. Scott reached over and kissed her husband on the cheek. He smiled and kissed her on the lips and she blushed like a school girl.

Mary thought they were about to leave when Michael took her hand; but they walked to the middle of the dance floor. The Maître d handed him a cordless microphone and he began talking.

Mary was completely caught off guard when he introduced her to the whole room as his future wife. He placed a humongous diamond and emerald ring on her finger and turned her into his arms. He winked at her and they kissed as if the room was empty. The room exploded in applause and shouts of congratulations and cheers for them. She was speechless. She had no idea he was going to make an announcement about them tonight but apparently Mr. and Mrs. Scott knew about it. Mary was in total shock! She didn't even have time to get nervous. All she could do was grin like a child on Christmas morning as the tears ran down her face, making her makeup all but disappear.

He took her back to the table, and first Mrs. Scott hugged her tight and kissed her cheek, followed by a hug and kisses on both cheeks from Mr. Scott. Phillip hugged her, kissed her cheek and whispered, "You got a good one Mary; you make him happy and that makes his whole world happy." Mary bent down to kiss Mama Lou who completely ignored her and said, "Let me see the ring child!" With that, everyone at the table burst out laughing.

The night began to come to an end. The Scotts volunteered to take Mama Lou home and she readily agreed. Mary floated out of the restaurant on Michael's arm with both her heart and her stomach full and happy. She thought to herself, "I am so in love, I want to scream it to the heavens!" She thanked God over and over while she waited for Michael to get the coats. People made their way over to where the Scott party was standing to congratulate Mary but mostly to see the ring. It was the most exquisite ring she had ever seen. It was a five carat emerald cut diamond with alternating emerald and diamond baguettes on each side. Surrounding the center stone are round emeralds and diamonds, all set in platinum. When their car came, they got in and waved goodnight to everyone as they slowly rode off into the night.

Mary was sitting back with her eyes closed still reeling from Michael's announcement of their engagement and the beautiful ring, trying to grasp and process in her head what happened tonight. It all happened so fast. They had only known each other 6 days. Maybe this was his "going slowly" but it sure seemed fast to her! However, Mary knew in her heart that only God can navigate circumstances like this.

She opened her eyes and Michael was staring at her with a smile on his face. "Did I do good with the ring? I wasn't sure about the size, but I heard ring and shoe size are the same so I guess that's true."

She stretched out her hand while saying, "My shoe size huh?" as they both looked at it, "I love it Michael! It is absolutely the most beautiful thing I have ever seen in my life. Fan-tab-u-lous! And it's a perfect fit. When in the world did you have time to do all of this? I mean, purchase clothes and accessories for me and Mama plus choose this spectacular ring in less than 24 hours?" she asked, in complete awe of him. He had truly worked an astonishing miracle and Mary loved him even more for the Herculean effort she knew it must've been.

He only winked and said, "What's the use of having millions if you can't make things happen when you need them to happen?"

"Thank you so much, Michael. This has been an amazing night and I promise you I will never forget it. Now, come here and let me kiss you the way you need to be kissed."

He pressed a button and the screen behind the driver went up, giving them total privacy. Soothing jazz was coming through the limo speakers. He took her into his arms and they kissed and kissed until they had to come up for air. Mary kissed his lips, his eyelids, his nose, his dimpled chin and his smooth cheeks.

Michael kissed her neck and shoulders. He kissed the tops of her breasts that were just peeking over the top of her dress. Mary whimpered and he lifted her face to him. While he kissed her, he slowly lowered the zipper on her dress and her breast slowly came into full view. He took one in each hand and put them in his mouth. They groaned together and she reclined in the seat. Michael got to his knees and continued to kiss and suckle her breast. Mary was about to explode and needed a diversion so she went for his belt. He moved her hands and explained to Mary this was her night.

He lifted her right leg up and kissed the inside of her knee. She wore sheer thigh high hose and he was thrilled. He placed her foot in the seat with her knee bent. Her dress had hidden his face from her. She felt his breath on her stomach and then he lifted her bottom to remove her panties. They were the same color as the dress. He brought them to his face and said, "Beautiful. You take my breath away". After he inhaled her panties, he put them in his pocket.

Mary was on fire and could feel the moisture pooling between her legs. She was ready for almost anything. She knew they would not have an intercourse so she believed that he would touch her with his fingers which would have sent her over the top. But she was not expecting what happened next. Michael raised her from the seat and put his mouth to the core of her womanhood and kissed her like he was kissing her mouth. He used his tongue and his lips to taste her essence. He tongued and sucked until he brought her to one gigantic mind-blowing orgasm. She shuttered and held on to his head while her essence was being drained from her. She felt like she was free-falling with no ground to catch her. Michael held her and continued to lick her until she was limp, very nearly unconscious.

He lowered her to the seat and took her face in his hands and looked into her eyes. "Mary Elizabeth Cross," he said, "I love you more than life itself. I love everything about you. I love the way you look; your smile; your smell; your taste; the way your skin feels; the way you move; your personality; everything. You make me happy just being near you. I will be counting the hours until we can be one. I want to love you the way you have never been loved. I want to show you what it's like to be loved by the soul mate God made especially for you. Do you understand me, Mary?"

Then he said something that completely blew her away and had her juices flowing all over again, "Taste and see how sweet you really are. I love it." His lips slowly descended on her lips and he kissed her with such a gentle touch that she moaned; or was it him? She was not really sure but it was unreal how much she loved Michael at that very moment.

When they parted, she saw tears in his eyes. Mary took her thumbs and wiped his face. She could only imagine how he was feeling; overjoyed, overwhelmed, and super stimulated. He leaned back against the seat and closed his eyes. At that moment, she was so in love with Michael Scott, only death could keep her from being his wife. She leaned over him and rested her head on his chest. His heart was beating a lot slower than hers. She noticed, for the first time how his manhood had made a wet spot in his pants. He was hard and pulsing. She knew he was in pain. She opened his pants and touched his hard penis with her fingers. He was hot to the touch. She slowly released his erection from his pants and then she kissed the wet tip of it. He tried to sit up and Mary gently pushed him down. "It's my turn Giant. Please be fair. This is not my night, this is our night."

He stretched out and Mary pushed his pants and black boxers down to his ankles which was quite a chore with his penis being in the state it was in. She got on her knees and kissed the head of his velvet steel rod once again. He moaned as she licked the head and sucked along the vein while she gently massaged his heavy sacs. She put him into her mouth and began to suckle him while she rubbed him up and down. She could feel him throb and jerk. She knew it wouldn't be long before she gave him a much-needed release. He held her head and pumped up as she went down on him. The speed increased and she reached up and rubbed his nipples through his shirt. He called out her name and went rigid. His essence flowed into her mouth and down her throat while she continued to rub and love on him. When the flow ended, he helped her up and into his arms. They kissed and held each other without speaking. Their bodies were doing all the communicating they needed. Finally, they silently rearranged themselves and tried to look like they had earlier, but they knew they didn't succeed. Mary didn't have on any panties and her hair most definitely was out of order and needed to be picked or patted into some reasonable shape. Michael lowered the screen and told Leon to take them to Mary's home. They rode the remaining distance hugging, squeezing, touching and kissing.

They came into the house and Michael made a fire. He went into "his" room and came out wearing his robe and pajama pants. Mary put on her pajamas and a robe also. They sat on the sofa and got comfortable. She was thinking about getting up for church. She didn't feel guilty, like she thought she would, but she felt like everyone would see her guilt on her face.

Michael was thinking about how waiting until June to marry this woman would probably kill him. He would be so crazy with need by the time June came that he could probably lift steel beams with his manhood.

Mary was thinking that she had been a juicy mess and she was a little embarrassed. But Michael knew she had not been with a man in almost 25 years. She was bound to have a lot of free flowing wetness. She thought, to herself and smiled, "He's just the man to help get some of that moisture out of me. After all, he started it flowing anyway." She wondered what he thought about it. Michael spoke first. "Sweet angel, do you believe that I love you with all my heart?"

"Of course I believe it. Why do you ask?"

"Well," he continued, "after this sweet preview of how our lovemaking will be, and after tasting you and your incredible sweetness which I absolutely love, there is no way in hell I am going to wait until June. No way; absolutely no way. Now what do you have to say?"

Mary rose up off him and replied, "I agree Michael. I don't want this to be any harder on us than it has to be. So, what do we do?"

He thought about it for a few minutes and declared, "Since we haven't told anyone except Mama Lou about the June 3rd date, it should be just a simple matter of getting the February 14th date booked at the church and at Foxwoods or the Convention Center. We haven't ordered invitations so that's not a problem. Let me get the place for the reception reserved and you secure Shiloh and Pastor Caldwell for the wedding. Once we do that, we can get the invitations done and you and the ladies can order the flowers, select your gowns, and anything else you want.

He made it sound so simple. Mary certainly hoped it would be that smooth. For sure she knew it would be wonderful, no matter what the wedding date would be. She agreed. They would simply move the date from June 3 to February 14. They sealed the deal with a long thrilling kiss. She curled up in his arms and soon they drifted off to sleep.

CHAPTER 7

✦✦✦✦✦

Sunday, November 23

Sunday morning, Mary opened her eyes to find herself in her bed alone. She rolled over and looked at the clock and it was 7:30. She wondered where Michael was and figured he had left sometime during the night. She closed her eyes and smiled remembering last night and how she was welcomed into a whole new world. She held her hand up and looked at her exquisite engagement ring. She whispered a prayer of thanksgiving to God and asked for forgiveness for letting her flesh over rule her head. She felt like God understood and would allow them to marry quickly so they wouldn't burn with sexual desire for each other.

She slowly sat up and in the midst of her stretch she realized someone was in the shower across the hall. That brought a smile to her face. Michael was still here. She opened her door and heard his baritone voice singing "I love You, I love You, I love You Lord today. Because You care for me in such a beautiful way, that's why I praise You, I lift You up, I magnify Your name. That's why my heart is filled with praise."

Mary got up smiling and humming the same praise song as she prepared to shower. She finished quickly and put on her underwear, hose and housedress. As she headed for the kitchen suddenly giant arms came up from behind her and she felt her heart dance. Michael turned her around and said, "Good morning beautiful". She said, "Good morning my handsome giant." They had a long loving kiss that said all was well with them. Michael sat at the island as Mary began to make breakfast. Just then, the doorbell rang. Michael said, "I'll get it. I'm expecting Leon." Mary didn't understand, but she continued to stir the waffle batter and tend to the bacon on the stove.

Michael went to the door and then down the hall to his room. He returned to his seat at the kitchen island grinning. "I had Leon bring me some clothes for church and something to put on later and some clothes for work tomorrow. Also, I had him to bring my briefcase, lap top and a car."

Mary said, "Oh, so I guess I have a house guest for the weekend" and she smiled and added "and he will be driving his own chariot too."

Michael laughed, "Well, I'm sorry I didn't ask first, but it's extremely hard to leave you Mary Elizabeth. I probably should have asked if it would be okay last night before we went to sleep, but I was already here and it just felt like the place where I belonged."

Mary walked to stand between his legs and reached up and touched his face. "Michael Scott, I was so pleased to hear you singing in the shower when I woke up this morning; even though I don't remember how I got in bed last night. We do belong together and I always want you near. So I guess we'd better eat so we can make it to church by 11:00." She kissed him quickly and returned to her cooking.

Michael set the table and Mary had him to play some of her favorite Gospel CDs. They ate shortly and breakfast was good and filling. They had waffles, bacon and eggs, fruit and coffee. While they were lingering over their coffee, Michael asked if he could pray. Mary's heart swelled and she nodded her accent. He took her hands, they bowed their heads and Michael prayed and thanked God for putting them together. He thanked God for making them for each other. He asked forgiveness for them getting out of control last night. He asked God to allow them to wed on Valentine's Day and he promised that he would try to refrain from getting so physical with Mary. Before he finished, Mary added her thanksgiving for Michael. She also asked God to protect their hearts from the arrows of jealousy and envy. She asked that he protect them from hurt or harm and to bless and keep their families. She asked God to keep their love strong and exciting. She promised they would be an addition to His kingdom that they would be lamps that light the way for others to follow.

At 10:45, when Michael pulled in to the parking lot at Shiloh Baptist Church they could hardly find a place to park. He came around to open the door for Mary and she blushed. Her hand kept him from bending down and kissing her right there in the church parking lot. They were both smiling as they approached the entrance.

Mary was greeted by the members in vestibule but the women were all smiling and looking at Michael. She introduced him to two of her friends, Lois Jones and Billie Fisher. Both the women were so awestruck looking at Michael, they shook hands but never stopped looking at him nor did they ever close their mouths. They didn't even notice Mary's ring she was trying to flash.

She said, "Ladies, I'm having fried crocodile toes for dinner this evening with tadpole gravy and molasses covered bat wings for dessert. I hope you two can come by." They both nodded and said they'd be there, never asking what time and never taking their eyes off Michael. As they walked away, Michael looked at Mary and she grinned, "See what you do to these women at Shiloh. I'd better hurry and get you married or you might get man-napped." They both laughed. He put his hand in the small of her back as she lead the way down the aisle to her favorite pew.

Michael sang during the praise and worship period. He wasn't shy nor did he appear to be uncomfortable. He had his Bible that was worn like Mary's. That let Mary know he was the kind of man she wanted. He was not ashamed to let people know that he was a child of God and he certainly knew how to pray. He apparently read his Bible even if he did not study God's word on a regular basis.

After service, Michael made his way through the congregation to Pastor Caldwell. Mary introduced him and the Pastor made a comment about Mary's ring. She blushed and Michael said, "Pastor, I plan to marry this angel of a woman on Valentine's Day. Mary was going to contact you about performing the ceremony for us, but since we're here now, we'd like to ask you to officiate at our wedding on February 14."

Pastor Caldwell hugged Mary and gave Michael a handshake with a pat on the back. He said it would be his pleasure to marry them. Then he said, "I've been wondering what was wrong with the single men at this church and why one of them hadn't grabbed up this angel."

Michael laughed and said, "Well Pastor, let me help you with that. She's MY angel, specially made by God for me. He kept her for me until we were both ready. Then He put me in the right place at the right time to meet and fall in love with the soul mate He made for me. He closed the other brothers' eyes to the real Mary. Then God took her desire for a companion away. She had to wait for me to get to her. Now I'm here and the rest is history."

"Well, that's the answer to my question then. I am certainly happy for both of you. Shall I look forward to having you become a part of the Shiloh family, Mr. Scott?"

"It certainly looks that way Pastor. I haven't been a member of a church in many, many years. But Shiloh feels good. I think it will be a good fit. Not only that, but if this is angel's home, then this is exactly where I am supposed to be, especially since I have no ties to any other church.

"I enjoyed the message this morning Pastor, and I look forward to hearing many more" he said. They said their goodbyes as he took Mary's arm and began to move her back up the aisle toward the vestibule.

Pastor Caldwell called after them, "We'll be happy to welcome you Brother Scott. Enjoy your day, both of you. You two make a mighty handsome couple."

Neither Michael nor Mary was very hungry, so they decided to go home and change clothes first, and wait until later to decide where to have lunch.

After they changed, they decided to eat a light lunch at home and then go out later for dinner. They played several hands of gin rummy and talked about the upcoming holidays and their traditions as well as wedding mistakes they would NOT make at their wedding. They laughed and talked until their stomachs told them it was time to eat something.

Together, they chopped the vegetables and shredded the potatoes and were sitting down to eat within 45 minutes. They had southwestern omelets and hash browns. For dessert they had ice cream and cookies.

Mary had been thinking about the holidays a lot. She didn't know what to do about her children and their families this week. They always came home for Thanksgiving and spent the entire weekend, beginning early Thursday morning. She knew Michael wanted her to spend it with his family. Mary didn't want the Scotts to have to make room for her family too.

Her family wasn't huge, but they were big eaters and none of them were babies. Her oldest was Alford and his wife Katie and their 22 year old twins Karl and Karla; Her oldest daughter Karen and her husband Erick and their teens Craig 18, Damon 16 and Cynthia 15; and her youngest daughter Beverly and her husband Gary and their 20 year old twins Andrea and Andre and 16 year old Jeremy. They would all be expecting to have Thanksgiving at her house. So, Mary did what she always did and gave it to God in prayer and said, "Your will be done Father, not my will."

Early that evening, the phone rang and it was Mary's daughters, Karen and Beverly. They wanted to talk and asked what she was doing. She couldn't tell them she was stretched out on the sofa with her feet in the lap of their future stepfather. She smiled to herself and said the timing was perfect and she could talk. They called to ask whether she would be upset if they didn't come home for Thanksgiving.

She was surprised, a little hurt but relieved at the same time. She wanted to know what was going on. They told her that their kids wanted to do something different. They were teenagers and young adults with plans for the long weekend. Both sets of twins who were in college, wanted to shop the early sales Friday morning. The other four worked in various department stores part-time and wanted to work early morning Black Friday for overtime pay. Mary realized that for young people, earning their own money was important. Heck, it was important to their parents too.

Her girls assured her that they would be there for New Year's instead and wanted to know if that would work. She wanted to know if their brother Al had been consulted and they said he had. They both started laughing and saying that his children were the ones who asked about skipping the Thanksgiving tradition this year. Of course, Alford did not know how to tell his mother, so he called his sisters and put them up to calling. Mary knew that sounded just like her son. He would never do anything that he thought might hurt his mother's feelings.

She told them she was glad they called because she had something she needed to discuss with them. This was perfect timing and since they wouldn't be there Thanksgiving she would discuss it with them now. Before she could get started, they started asking questions about her health. Is something wrong with the house? Was she having financial problems? When they finally let her talk, she told them she had met her soul mate, he had proposed, and they were getting married on Valentines' Day.

There was silence and then they started in with questions, which she stopped. "Listen to me carefully. I was married to your father for 20 years and we had a wonderful marriage. He's been gone for almost 24 years. I have met my soul mate and we both knew we were meant to be together almost the moment we met. He is a good man; a God-fearing man who loves me and has shown his love for me in so many, beautiful ways. We have not been intimate; but, we are not going to be tempted to break God's laws by dragging out our courtship. He loves me and wants to marry me just like I am. He has his own place and his own money. As a matter of fact, he's got more money than we can spend in a lifetime. So, just know that I will be in good hands. Oh, hold on, he wants to say something."

Michael said, "Hello, Karen and Beverly. I'm Michael Scott and I am so in love with your mother, my angel, I can hardly believe it myself, because I have never been in love or married before. She has talked about you two and Alford and she didn't know how to tell you about us. We're glad you called today. God intervened for us so your call was perfectly timed. I can't wait to meet all three of you in person. Your mother is the only woman I have ever loved and I have known a lot of women. But understand this. When God makes your soul mate, you recognize each other instantly. You can't explain the love and you certainly don't expect the love. But when it happens, it is undeniable and all the people around you can see and feel the love too. The people around us know we're in love and they are happy for us. So, I'm glad to get to talk with you. Now, you ladies be careful and stay safe. Here's your mother."

There was silence on the phone. Mary said, "Are you all there?"

Finally, Beverly said, "Ah, Mama we are just in shock! We'll let you go and we'll talk to you later."

"Well, alright ladies. Kiss my sons and grandchildren."

They said they would and then the line went dead. Mary thought to herself, Alford will call early in the morning. Michael smiled and kissed her nose. Well, that went well, he thought. Only Mary knew that the fall-out wouldn't start until Alford got the news. Before they could get comfortable again, the phone rang.

Mary answered and she heard, "Mama! What on earth are you thinking? You can't get married. You'll lose Dad's social security and his veterans' benefits. Then what are you going to do. Be dependent on some man to take care of you. No way, Mama! What's gotten in to you? You aren't thinking right."

Mary put the phone on speaker so Michael could hear, "Hello to you too, son. First of all, I know that. Second, will you calm down and stop talking so loud?"

After a moment, he said, "Sorry, Mama. How are you doing?"

"I'm doing great Son. How are you? How is Katie? How are the twins?"

He answered her questions and it helped him to calm down.

Finally, he said, "Mom, when did you meet this man?"

"November 17th. Mary responded. Why?" She knew he was concerned about her being used.

And after he stated his concerns, she said, "Listen to me, son. I am old enough to know what love is. I love this man and he loves me. We are sure, and we both feel that God made us for each other. I tell you what. Why don't you come up sometime this weekend so you two can meet?" He agreed and said he'd be there Saturday. She looked at Michael and he nodded his agreement.

They ended the call with her son saying, "I love you, Mama. Please be careful."

Michael said, "I like him. He's concerned and doesn't mind expressing his feelings. We're going to get along fine."

Mary had no doubt that he would eventually like all her children. The hard part was going to be getting past this awkward period. They hugged and kissed and decided it was time to get out of the house. They were both deep in thought as they left the house to go for a ride.

CHAPTER 8

Thursday, November 27

Thanksgiving at the Scotts' house was steeped in years of traditions and in full swing. They always ate at Michael's house in the large formal dining room. They always invited all the relatives who lived in and around the Hartford-New York area. Mama Lou and Mary spent the night so they could be up early to help with all the preparations. The dining room table could seat 24, which was good, because there was seldom less than ten or twelve out of town guests plus the close local friends who were like family. Now that their circle included two more, the table was set for 22 adults and a side table for 7 children, all under the age of 12.

The men were enjoying football in the theater room and the older children were in the game room. The younger children were being kept busy by the older girls. The ladies were all bustling around between the kitchen and the dining room, getting this year's preferred linens out, gathering enough serving dishes to go on the table, getting the center pieces from the butler's pantry, setting the table and making sure that there were enough places for the children. They were all busy, laughing and talking and Mary was enjoying being a part of it all. Even Mama Lou fell right in line. She was in the kitchen on a stool, rolling out rolls and brushing butter on them. There were so many desserts Mary was already finding it hard to decide which one to eat first. Mama Lou and Mrs. Scott were baking the homemade rolls which had the whole house smelling like a bakery. Every few minutes one of the guys would come down to ask, "Are the rolls ready yet?" to which the women answered, "NO!"

At 2:30 everything was ready. Everyone gathered around the table and held hands while Mr. Scott blessed the food. He made special mention of Mary and Mama Lou being a part of their family and he prayed for Michael and Mary's impending union. When he said amen, everyone settled into their places and the feast began! The food was delicious and everyone thoroughly enjoyed the meal and the conversation.

When the last plate of dessert was consumed, the table was cleared and everyone moved to various places throughout the house to relax and take a nap. Michael and Mary went outside and took a walk. The air was chilled, but the sky was clear and the wind was not blowing. They stopped and sat down on a bench near the entry to the back yard. Michael reached for her and she eased into his arms without a word. She looked at him and he seemed troubled. She knew he would tell her what was on his mind when he was ready. He had to decide first how to say whatever it was, so she waited. She kissed him on his cheek and he smiled and kissed her nose. He took a step away from her and turned, "Mary Elizabeth, I love you so much until sometimes it scares me. The things we did to each other in the limo the other night, still bother me. You are a very passionate woman, and I know you enjoy giving and receiving love. I understand you because you are the female side of me." He paused and came back and knelt in front of her. She had no idea where he was going with this conversation.

"Sweetheart, if we are ever alone again, I don't think I will be able to just kiss and love on you like that. I want all of you. I want to be inside you and feel your insides grab and squeeze me. I want to be deep inside you when my essence explodes in you. Do you understand what I'm trying to say?"

She knew exactly what he was getting at. She had been thinking about that night in the limo too. She felt that they really did come close to breaking her vow and she didn't want them to do that.

"What I'm saying is this." He continued. "I will not be able to be alone around you very much from now until February 14th. I'm going to get real busy, maybe even work on some overseas projects and for sure I'm going to have to leave Connecticut."

Mary couldn't keep silent any longer. "Michael, please don't run from this. We have to trust God and know that He will protect us and keep us from ourselves. Running only adds the possibility of plane and car accidents, and time that the enemy can use to throw monkey wrenches into our plans. Please just trust God and be still and let Him keep us free from sexual sin."

Michael walked away and stood several minutes looking out over the white pristine snow. She knew he heard what she said. She only hoped that he would take heed. He turned around and opened his arms and she came to him. Then she knew he understood. He held her close and his warmth spread through her like standing in front of an open fire.

He kissed the top of her head and said, "Thanks Sweetheart, for reminding me that my Father in heaven provides a way out of temptation. The Holy Spirit just reminded me that, *"greater is He that is in you, than he that is in the world." (New American Standard Bible, 1 John 4:4)* Thank you, angel for your love and your trust. If you trust that we can do this, then I believe we can also. Now kiss me and let's seal the deal."

Mary laughed and they did seal the deal with a sweet loving kiss. Michael took out his phone and shortly looked at her and said, with a big grin, "Seventy-nine days and counting!" Mary said, "That means we have eleven weeks and 2 days to pull a wedding together. Thank God for your mother and Phillip!" she said in awe, as the gravity of the whole thing started to settle over her.

CHAPTER 9

+ + + + + +

November 28

After talking at length to Mrs. Scott, she agreed to help Mary select her gown, accessories and the gowns for the wedding party. They decided to have breakfast Saturday morning and discuss everything before hitting the stores. She would be at Mary's house at 8 o'clock. Mary worked on everything from the color scheme to the kind of flowers she wanted to use. She didn't have any one particular friend to serve as a bridesmaid; so, she wanted to ask Mama Lou because she was her best friend. The ring bearer and flower girl would be some of Michael's cousins because her own grand children were teens and young adults. They would be hostesses and ushers along with the other children on the Scott side.

Both Mary's parents were deceased and no one needed to give her away. After all, she was sixty years old. She figured she could give her own self away. She secretly wished that her son would walk her down the aisle, but she would not ask him.

She liked the colors silver and charcoal with red as the accent color. She wanted the wedding to begin at 11am and the reception at 12noon. She didn't want a sit down reception or a plated meal, just cake, punch and the cake cutting, champagne toast and then she and Michael could be off to places unknown by 2:00pm. They did not want gifts but she didn't know how to tell the guests that. She went to the library and looked at bridal magazines to see how people handled telling their friends not to buy any wedding gifts.

Later that day she went to the fabric store to look at patterns of wedding dresses. She knew it would be hard to find something that would suit

Mama Lou just right. But she had no idea how many bridal books and helpful hints there were on the internet. When she finally went to bed Friday evening, she had a headache just thinking about all the decisions that had to be made.

She was drifting off to sleep when the phone rang. Mary looked at the clock and it was almost eleven. She knew it was Michael. They talked briefly and he kept reminding her that she had the final say so on all the decisions about the wedding. He told her not to let his mom or anyone try to get her to do something that she didn't want to do. They joked about the white shoes and ended the call with vows of love and longing. Sleep finally came and it was full of dreams of cruise ships, oceans, snow-capped mountains and sunny beaches.

Michael rolled over after talking with Mary and sighed. Oh, how he wanted her in his bed. He marked off a calendar he had hidden in his nightstand. Seventy eight days to go. He wondered if Mary would let his mother force her to do things that were uncomfortable. He wanted this wedding to be exactly what Mary wanted it to be. Not something his mother had dreamed up to impress their family and friends. He only wished the wedding was tomorrow and not in distant February.

He needed to talk to his father about how to get out from under so much of the day to day operations of the company. After all, he was 62 and most people his age were already thinking about retiring. Funny, he had never thought about it until he met his angel. He was content to work and go home to an empty house; work and have some woman meet him for dinner who he knew would willingly satisfy his physical needs; work and buy whatever he saw that he wanted for whomever he wanted to give it to and work some more.

Now, he wanted Mary Elizabeth in his home when he got home from work; she's the one he wanted to share a meal with and then his bed; she was the person he wanted to buy things for and then watch her eyes light up when he gave them to her. Yes, no doubt about it. She was his woman and he was as sure of that as he was that tomorrow was Saturday.

Saturday morning dawned gray and rainy. Mary was dressed and having a cup of tea before 7:30. She made a coffee cake this morning and fried some extra bacon to serve Mrs. Scott with some coffee or tea. She figured she would have probably just had coffee before rushing out on this rainy morning.

When her bell sounded at 7:40 she was startled. She opened the door to the smiling face of her giant. Her body responded like he had been away for a month when she had just seen him Thursday evening. They hugged and kissed and she took his coat and put it in the closet.

"What on earth are you doing here, and so early?"

Michael smiled and took her hand and led her into the dining room. He sat at the table and pulled her into his lap." Well, I remembered that you and Mom were going shopping today and I needed to bring you something." He reached inside his jacket pocket and took out a leather document holder.

"Michael," she began before he could put it on the table.

"Hold on, angel, before you start in on me. I need you to listen first and then ask questions. Okay?"

"Okay." she said.

"Good. These are credit cards that I want you to use for the wedding expenses. I have already ordered yours in your name and until they come, use these. This is a certified letter giving you the authority to use them. It doesn't matter which one you use. There are no limits on any of them so get whatever you want. Please don't worry about the money. I have it to spend and I need you to understand that I do not want you to scrimp or be conservative with any aspect of this wedding. Do you understand? In other words, it doesn't have to be on sale for you to buy it. If you see it and you want it, buy it!"

Mary just nodded her head, unshed tears in her eyes. She knew Michael was wealthy, but she could not imagine having credit cards with no limits. This giant of a man loved her and was putting it all out there for her and the world to see. She put her arms around his neck and he breathed in her scent. He was instantly turned on. He slid his hands up and down her back and he felt her shiver.

He stood up and lifted her chin, "Mary, please don't let any part of planning for this wedding stress you out. Do it just like you want and spend whatever it cost. Agreed?"

"I love you Michael."

"Agreed?" Michael asked again. Mary answered yes as she wiped her face on her apron. The doorbell sounded as he was putting on his coat. He went to the door and greeted his surprised but smiling mother. "Good morning, Mom!" He said cheerfully as he bent to kiss her cheek.

"Good morning, son." she said.

He turned and kissed Mary quickly her on the lips, "Bye love."

Mary kissed him back and he was out the door.

"That boy never ceases to amaze me. I just waved at him this morning as he was leaving. I thought he was going to the office."

"Let's begin again, shall we? Hello Mary. It's good to see you."

"Hello Mama Dot. I'm glad to see you also. I'm glad you're here." Mary hung up her coat and walked with her into the dining room. After they sat down, Mary remembered the bread and fruit. "I made some coffee cake and fruit and bacon and eggs if you would care for some."

Dorothy grinned and responded, "I didn't eat this morning because I thought we'd have breakfast out. But this is so much better. I would love to share breakfast with you. What can I do?" she asked.

Mary asked her to get the placemats out of the cabinet and the plates were already out on the island in the kitchen. They began to get things ready for their meal and talked as if they were old friends. They both were thinking how much they genuinely liked each other. Mary called Mama Lou to come over and she did.

After a lovely breakfast, they cleared the table and began talking about the wedding. They continued to talk and Mama Lou took notes. They settled on the colors and Mama Lou was so surprised to be asked to be her matron of honor. If only all the decisions could be made that simply. Mary knew the smooth ride would not last long and she thought she was prepared for it. But little did she know that the battle would be whether to take the wedding from simple and classic to enormous and extravagant.

They invited Mama Lou to go along with them since she had the notes from their discussion. Plus, it would be good to get her gown selected as soon as possible and remove one sure headache off the table. When she went home to lock her house, Mrs. Scott and Mary tidied the kitchen. Mrs. Scott was amazed at how domestic Mary was. The fact that she cooked cakes and pies from scratch and preferred eating at home to eating out really impressed her. It reminded her of the time when she used to bake from scratch and cook every day for Jack and Michael. She wondered whether she could still do it. She decided she would just have to go in the kitchen one day and see what she could do. No doubt Jack would be very appreciative of her skills. She thought he would never stop raving about her blackberry cobbler.

Mary thought she was driving, but a black Lincoln town car was sitting in the driveway when she opened the door to leave. She decided that on a day like today, she could really appreciate not having to drive.

They decided to go to an upscale mall to look for Mama Lou's dress or suit. Leon let them out and Dorothy told him she'd call when they were ready. He drove off and Mary wondered where he would be while he waited for them. What would he be doing? Had he eaten breakfast?

They entered a shop and were immediately met by the store owner and two sales assistants. Mrs. Scott made the introductions to the owner. Mary was introduced as Michael's fiancée and they were looking for a dress or suit for the bride's matron of honor. They were ushered into a room with a sofa and several chairs.

The ladies helped Mama Lou look at several gowns and elegant suits before she saw one she wanted to try. It was too big; the next one was too long; the third one was not stylish enough and Mrs. Scott agreed with her about each one of them. The clerks brought out a rack of dresses and everyone chose several for her to try. She finally settled on a satin charcoal dress with beads on the skirt that was tea length and full. It had a short sleeved sheer embroidered jacket. The dress looked gorgeous on Mama Lou and it had just enough bling to keep it from being dull.

Mrs. Scott saw a lovely gray crepe dress with a shawl collar and a straight skirt. It was embellished with pearls and had a lovely organza bow on the side. She tried it on and she looked stunning. She chose it without any hesitation. The dresses were to be delivered to Mrs. Scott's house. Mary almost choked when she saw the bill, but she signed the sales receipt and put her copy in her empty coupon holder. Mary recovered after having a talk with herself about doing what Michael said. She had just spent $2400 for two dresses and they weren't even hers! She thanked the Lord for Michael's kind heart.

Next, they went to a bridal shop that specialized in designer gowns. She had no idea what kind of dress she wanted or whether she wanted a suit or an after five dress. Again Mrs. Scott introduced them and they were ushered into a dressing room more stylish than the last one. They were offered champagne, which neither of them accepted. The store owner came out, followed by two assistants. One had a tape measure around her neck and the other had belts and several single shoes. After measuring everything on Mary except the length of her afro, they led her to the center of the room and up on a round platform which was slowly raised about two feet off the floor. Mary was startled but tried to remain calm. They asked her questions about the kind of dress she wanted and she answered as best she could.

After the grilling ended, the owner and sales assistants left the room and returned shortly with a rack of six gowns. When Mary saw them she wanted to scream. Did she look like a woman who would wear a Barbie Doll looking wedding gown, with ruffles and 20 yards of tulle? One glance at their first selections and she quickly said no. They left immediately and returned with another rack of six dresses. These were less bouffant but still not what she wanted. The third rack had some that looked promising. However, upon closer examination these dresses were either too low in the front or the back, or there was a split from the floor to thigh. Mary is not a modest woman, but she is a sixty ear old woman. There are some parts of her anatomy that will only be revealed to her husband, and only in private.

They were getting tired wanted a change. Mary asked Mama Dot if she had ever eaten in The Russell Restaurant downtown and she hadn't so that's where they headed for lunch. Mama Lou knew about the place because Mary had bought her jerk chicken sandwiches when she was in the area. Of course she started talking about how good the food was and they heard Mrs. Scott's stomach growl which gave them all the giggles. No sooner had they stopped laughing when Mary's stomach did the same thing. They started laughing all over again. As they got out of the car, Leon had the strangest expression on his face.

Mama Lou said to him, "It's called 'laughter'. You should try it sometimes; it's good medicine for the soul, my boy!" They agreed with her. Mary invited him to come in and have some lunch. He declined, so she decided to have a sandwich and chips with a drink delivered to him at the car. Lunch was fun and a great pick me up for the ladies. Mama Dot picked up a matchbook from the restaurant as they were leaving. She said she was coming back with Jack one day. She loved the food. After lunch, as Mary was getting in the car, Leon winked at her and mouthed 'Thank you'. She winked back at him and mouthed, 'You're so welcome'.

Mama Lou said she wanted to go home now because she was tired. They took her home and helped her get settled. They left her shortly after 2pm and headed back out for more shopping. Mary had seen a bridal shop on LaSalle in West Hartford. She asked Leon to take them there. It was a small rather charming little store. She introduced herself and Mama Dot to the woman who came from the back of the store when the little bell rang over the door. She asked Mary what she had in mind and she told her that she really didn't have anything in mind. She just knew what she didn't want.

The woman listened attentively as Mary told her the wedding colors and her age. She went to the back of the store and returned with two dresses. One was ivory with Chantilly lace and beautiful vintage pearls, sequins and rhinestones. It was a lovely dress, but it had a fishtail bottom and Mary didn't want that. It was also long sleeves. When she saw the second dress she immediately knew it would be hers. It was a dark gray lace over satin charcoal dress with the collar that folded down over the shoulders; it was fitted to just below the knee where it was slightly flair; the horizontal ruche front and back started from underneath the collar and ended where the flair began. It was exactly what she could see herself wearing; elegant and unique. Mary went to try it on and it fit like a glove. She gasped when she saw her reflection in the mirror.

Mama Dot said, "That's it! No doubt about it! I love it on you! Michael is going to flip when he sees you walking down the aisle!"

Mary turned around a couple more times and told the shop owner, can you have this delivered?"

She beamed, "Of course; my pleasure!"

Mary had just spent $2800, but this time, it felt good and no guilt. Next, they went to Mary's favorite shoe store where she found the perfect shoes. Mama Dot found a perfect pair of shoes and a bag to go with her dress.

They ended their shopping and made a date to start looking at invitations Wednesday. Mrs. Scott asked Mary whether she had started on her invitation list and of course she had not even thought about it. Mary told her she would work on it over the weekend. She promised she would have her list Wednesday.

Mary dreaded working on the list because that meant making sure she had addresses for all her invitees. Plus she had to get in touch with those she kept in touch with via email and the phone. She suddenly felt exhausted just thinking about it and decided to work on her email contacts first.

Chapter 10

November 29

She called Michael after taking a relaxing shower. He had just made it home. They talked about their day and Mary shared how much she had gotten done. He said he knew she must be worn out, but he reminded her that Alford was supposed to meet them this evening.

Mary had forgotten when she heard her door open. "He's walking in the door now, Michael. Let me get dressed, see you soon." Michael changed his shirt, put on a sweater, grabbed his leather jacket and picked up his keys to the SUV.

Alford came into his mother's bedroom just as she was coming out of the bathroom. She had put on a colorful caftan and was smiling broadly at her firstborn child. He opened his arms to her and she went to him commenting on how good he looked. They left the bedroom and he was about to sit at the kitchen island when he got a good look at his mother.

"Mama, you look good. You're actually glowing. WOW!"

"Boy you act like you were expecting to see some other mama. I always look good, don't I?" she asked as she playfully hit him on the arm.

"Now you stop acting like you're brand new and sit down."

"How is the family?" They talked about his twins being home from college over the weekend. He said "Katie is fine, happy that the kids are home, but complaining about the twins bringing home their friends. Instead of two there are 6 youngsters in the house. Katie said they act like she's running a restaurant/lounge/ laundry/motor lodge.

Mary laughed, "I'll have to call her. Remind her that she only has two and thank God they are not the same sex. Can you imagine what it would be like if it was 6 girls or 6 boys in the house?"

"Yes I can. She'd probably move back to the Bronx for the weekend." He continued to share more about the twins and their antics. They laughed and remembered those days when he was working on his MBA. What a chaotic place the house was then.

The conversation got back around to his real purpose for coming home and he questioned his mother about her feelings for the man.

"What is it? Do you think people my age can't fall in love? Listen, son, I'm very happy for the first time in a very long time. I'm in love with a man who is beautiful both inside and out. He loves me unconditionally and he likes to make me happy. So try to wrap your mind around that. Okay?"

"God put us together and there's nothing you or anyone else can do about it. We didn't ask for it and we weren't looking for it. It just happened and we are both ecstatic about it. The end."

Alford was amazed at his mother's boldness. He had never heard her talk like this before. She asked if he was hungry and of course he said yes. Mary made turkey sandwiches. Just as she was about to make his plate, the doorbell rang. She said a prayer as she went to the door.

Michael came in the house and took her in his arms.

He said, "I missed you, angel."

"I missed you too, giant."

After a brief kiss, she took his coat as he walked into the kitchen and Alford stood up.

"Alford Cross," he said as he extended his hand to Michael, looking him over from head to toe, impressed with everything he saw.

"Michael Scott" he replied, grasping the young man's hand. He noticed how Alford was earnest, not timid and he had a firm strong grip. 'Nice', Michael thought. 'I knew I would like this young man'.

Mary came in the room and asked if he was hungry. He said always, but that he would grab something on the way home. Mary told him to sit and that she was just about to serve Alford.

As soon as he sat down, Alford asked him, "So you want to marry my mother, huh? Have you ever been married before? Do you know how to treat a wife?"

Before Michael could answer, he continued, "My mother has a heart the size of Texas. She's a busy person and you won't get to keep her at home all day cooking and cleaning. She's a giver; she's a doer."

Michael took a deep breath and then responded, "Alford, I have never been married, because I had not met my soul mate. As soon as I met your mother, I knew she was the woman God created for me. Yes, I know how to treat a wife. My parents have been married over 65 years and they are still happy and in love. I know she's a giver, because she gave me a future that I never dreamed I'd have. I have a maid and a cook at my place, so she won't have to do anything she doesn't want to do. I love her Alford, more than life itself, and I'll do anything humanly possible to make sure her wants and needs are met. She will want for nothing. I'll never intentionally hurt her. You have my word on that."

They ate the sandwiches and had a very relaxed conversation. They moved into the living room and Michael got in his spot and Mary got comfortable in her spot, the other end of the sofa with her feet in his lap. Alford observed them closely and sure enough, he saw and felt the love between this tall elegant man and his caring mother.

As he prepared to leave, he turned to them and said, "Well I wasn't sure how I would feel after this meeting, but I can honestly say that I'm satisfied. I can see that you two are very much in love. I can also tell that you were made for each other. You think alike to the extent that you finish each other's sentences. That's better than me and my wife and we've been married 23 years." He chuckled.

He kissed his Mama and gave Michael a man hug. He said he'd pass on the info to his sisters and he would see them New Year's Eve. While they were saying goodbye, Michael slipped on his coat. He told Mary he knew she was tired and he was going to go so she could get some rest. He said he'd pick her up for church. They kissed lovingly and he walked out with Alford.

The two men stood on the sidewalk for several minutes and had what looked like a serious talk. Alford walked Michael to his car and they continued to talk. Finally they shook hands again and Michael got in his SUV and drove away. Alford turned and went to his car and got in. He backed out of the driveway and waved at his mother whom he knew was still looking out the window. Mary turned off the interior light and headed to the kitchen. She cleaned up quickly and headed for bed for the second time that night.

As she was getting comfortable, she suddenly realized she couldn't meet with Mrs. Scott on Wednesday. They couldn't start until after 4pm when she left the library. Thursday she could meet, but it would have to be after 2pm when she finished at the church bookstore; or they could meet Friday after 12 when she finished her Bible study class at the nursing home; if all else failed, most of her Saturdays were free. She missed her water aerobics class this morning, but next time they would have to meet after her class around 11:30am. Mary decided to call her in the morning as soon as she got up.

Her phone rang and she knew it was Michael. He said, "Angel, do you realize that you spent a whole eight hours shopping for three dresses and two pairs of shoes?"

She laughed. "Yes, I know. Can you imagine how long it is going to take to select the menu, the cakes and the wine? Don't forget the flowers?"

"Michael, don't remind me of the work I have to do. I'm already on wedding overload. You are going to pay for this, and I don't mean with your credit card."

She could hear his smile when he said, "I'm looking forward to it. My debt will be paid in full! Get some rest. I appreciate all your hard work for our wedding. Just know that it will all pay off in the end. Rest well, sweetheart. Good night angel."

Mary smiled and snuggled in her bed. "You too love." She went to sleep with visions of scenes of her life with her future husband. She could only sigh as she thought about all the ways they could share their lives with each other.

Chapter 11

December 6

Mary changed the Wednesday appointment with Mama Dot to look at invitations and flowers to Friday at 1pm. Now she had more time to work on her invitation list. Dorothy felt they needed to have the list complete when they selected the invitations although Mary could not understand how the two were connected.

Friday when Mary left the Trinity Hill Care Center, she stopped by Mama Lou's for lunch before heading out for yet another wedding task. Selecting the flowers seemed to be really important to her future mother in-law.

The first florist happened to also specialize in one-of-a-kind invitations, which was great, or so Mary thought. But they could not seem to agree on any of the invitations they looked at. So they decided to go to another place that she wanted to show Mary. She felt like they would be sure to fine exactly what they wanted.

They made the final selection on the flowers, ribbon colors and specific arrangements for all the tables including the head table. They had selected the corsages and boutonnieres for the wedding party. Mary had just spent $16,000 on flowers. Just thinking about it made her dizzy. It was already after 3:30 and Mary was ready to go home. She was meeting Michael and they were looking forward to spending a quiet evening together.

They arrived at Mama Dot's favorite stationery shop and just walking in Mary knew immediately she was in for a battle. Mama Dot was greeted by a gentleman with a French accent who kissed her on both cheeks. He lifted Mary's hand and kissed it. They were led into a beautiful room with a large circular table which was surrounded by three very comfortable chairs.

Henri sat in the middle chair, the lights slowly dimmed while a screen was lowered from the ceiling. Henri took a remote control and clicked it at the screen. There, on this huge screen was an announcement of Mary and Michael's wedding with the incorrect information.

Mary turned to her left and said to Henri, "That is not correct. I don't like the lettering and the color is all wrong. Obviously this was just a sample to look at." She paused and continued, "So, do you have any others that I might see? My colors are black and charcoal with a hint of red. We can use a silver card as the charcoal, but definitely not an ivory invitation. Also, the correct location of the wedding is Shiloh Baptist Church."

She was interrupted when Mrs. Scott surprisingly said, in a rather condescending way, "Mary surely you can't be thinking of having your wedding at Shiloh. It's much too small. It's a bit run down don't you think?" she asked. "I suppose we could have the rehearsal dinner in the fellowship hall over at Shiloh if you want your church to be involved. We'll just need to get a cleaning service over there and spruce the place up a bit."

"When is the last time you were inside Shiloh, Mama Dot? It must have been a while. You should stop by one day and see how wrong you are about it."

Henri turned back to the computer and made the corrections to the location printed on the invitation. "Oh!" he said as he jumped up from the table, "I think I have an invitation that you will love. It is absolutely perfect."

He went to the door and spoke to his assistant quietly in rapid French. Mary said to Mama Dot, "How did the time change from 11am to 5pm? We have reasons for the time we selected. Why did you change it?"

She, looked directly into Mary's face and said, "I just think it would be better to have a late afternoon wedding. The tradition in" and Mary cut her off. "Mama Dot, this is my and Michael's wedding. We selected the time and the place and they are not negotiable."

Just then Henri stepped in and sat down. He handed Mary a shiny charcoal looking envelope. She opened it and inside, there was a piece of tissue paper that looked like black lace. "It is just like my dress!" she screamed and hugged Henri and kissed him on the cheek. "Look Mama Dot, isn't this just perfect! Thank you Henri!" Mama Dot smiled as she nodded her head. Yes, it was perfect.

Mary took Mama Dot's hand and asked Henri to give them a moment. After he left, Mary began, "Mama Dot, I don't mean to sound ugly or to upset you. I love Michael so much. We could go down to the court house one day at noon and I would be just as happy to be his wife. I realize that your family name has a certain reputation and a certain standard in everything associated with it. I don't want to do anything that would bring negative publicity to the family. All I'm saying is that this is my wedding. Michael and I have talked. He wants me to be satisfied with everything and so do I. Look at it this way. Why waste the whole day and wait until 5pm to be married. We don't want to wait a minute longer than absolutely necessary. I think he'd have the ceremony at 6am if I'd let him."

Mama Dot smiled. "I think I understand now. Let me ask you a very personal question. Are you and Michael abstaining from sexual intimacy while you're waiting to be married?" She lowered her head, hesitated a moment then looked up and said, "Yes." Mama Dot took Mary in her arms and said, "11 am sounds perfect to me too."

They called Henri who came into the room and saw that all was well. The location of the wedding, and the time were changed along with a more readable font. When he put it back up on the screen, with the selected invitation, it was perfect. They decided on the proper wording for the wedding only invitation, the wedding and reception invitation, as well as the invitation for the reception only and how many to order. After going over both their lists, the costs were calculated. For an extra charge, Henri would have the envelopes printed including the return address. He gave them a couple of weeks to finalize both lists. When they left, they were both happy. Michael was out of $9600. Mary wondered how much the food, music and rehearsal dinner was going to cost.

She made it home just after 5:15 to find Michael's car in her driveway. As she pulled her car into the driveway he called her from Mama Lou's. He ran over and kissed her and she literally did not want to let him go. She felt so safe and loved in his arms.

They stayed at Mama Lou's a while longer. Since she kept talking about Shorty's stuffed baked potatoes, they concluded that's what they would eat for dinner. Michael went to get them while Mary went home to take a quick shower and change clothes. She was startled when she opened her bathroom door and he was sitting on her bed, looking at her with that look that said, BEWARE. She pulled her robe a little tighter and came into the room. Michael stood up and walked over to her. He said her name and she melted in his arms. He held her and whispered his love in her ear while she trembled and wished they could make love right here on the floor in the middle of her bedroom.

He held her back and slowly untied the sash holding her robe open to his hungry eyes. He stared at her for what seemed like an hour. He turned and left the room. She heard the door close.

Whew! That was close, Mary thought! If he had asked her, Mary would not and could not have refused him. Of course he knew that, which is why he left. Mary's love for her giant just grew ten times more. She quickly dressed and went next door where he and Mama Lou were waiting. They ate and laughed and talked about everything and nothing. After cleaning up the table and putting the leftovers in the refrigerator, they said goodnight to Mama Lou.

Michael and Mary went over the day's purchases and he shook his head at how little she had spent. He kept asking her if she was sure she was getting what she wanted. Mary was absolutely amazed that money meant nothing to him. She guessed he was going to learn rather quickly that she could squeeze a George Washington until he cried uncle. She wasn't cheap, she was just economical. She was a bargain hunter. If it wasn't on sale, Mary didn't buy it; that is until she met Michael.

She tried to talk him into going with her to Foxwoods to select the lunch menu and he kept saying, "Get cheese and crackers and those little wieners on toothpicks. Let's cut the cake, do a toast get the hell out of Dodge. Baby, why do we have to do a full meal?"

She told him that his mother would not hear of anything else and to let it go. He kept grumbling about how long it would take to feed everyone and how everyone was going to want to talk and make toasts and do a lot of other things just to keep them away from each other longer. Mary told him she would do her best to get his mother to agree to a compromise. She gave him a kiss to jump start his heart and told him to be patient, there was more where that came from. He said, "Your debt count is going up angel; that's seven!"

CHAPTER 12

December 13

Mary went to the church to help with the Christmas Party for the girls' group she volunteered with. When she left she had her nails and toenails done. She and Michael were attending his company's Christmas gala and she was looking forward to it.

She was wearing the charcoal faux wrap dress with rhinestones. She wished she had a necklace to wear, but she didn't, so she was content to wear what she had, beautiful long earrings; a gift from her William, her first husband. She loved those earrings and thankfully they would be perfect with her beautiful designer dress.

She and Michael had talked about the dresses and he always told her to wear whichever one she wanted. He showed her which dress he guessed she would wear to dinner last month and he had picked the one she wore. She told him to guess again about tonight's attire. He said he would put it in his tux pocket. She was still surprised to know that he guessed right the first time. She was sure he couldn't do it twice, but she'd have to wait and see.

He was picking her up at 6:30 and she was ready except for putting on her shoes and her dress. The doorbell rang. She figured it was him. To her surprise it was Mama Lou. She usually came in the side door so Mary was curious.

Mama Lou said, "I almost forgot that I accepted this box for you this morning while you were at the church" she said handing Mary a box. They went into the dining room and Mama Lou sat down.

Mary asked, "Why didn't you use your key and come in the side door?"

Mama Lou looked down and said, "I can't find it. I know it's in the house somewhere, but for the life of me I can't find it anywhere. I have looked high and low. I'm sorry Mary. I hope it doesn't get into the wrong hands."

Mary smiled and told her not to worry. Until she found it, she would keep the safety lock on the door just in case. Mama Lou looked relieved and sat back in the chair.

Mary opened the long box and found a smaller one inside. Mary opened it and almost fell down. Mama Lou got up to see and she clutched at her heart.

"Is that real?" she asked almost in a whisper. Mary looked up and turned the box top over; it was from Nordstrom's.

"It's real Mama Lou."

Michael had enclosed a card which read, 'This is how you make my eyes shine when I look at you. I love you Mary Elizabeth. May I have the honor or placing this gem on my angel's neck this evening?'

Mary lifted the necklace out of the box and looked at it with tears streaming down her face. She turned and ran into the bathroom and thanked God for giving her to Michael and for his love for her. She repaired her make-up and finished getting dressed. She looked at her earrings and decided to remove them. Instead, she put on a pair of diamond studs that she had owned for many years. They were perfect; small but perfect. She eased her earrings back in the box and put them in her jewelry box.

She came out and Mama Lou was sipping some tea. "Sweetie, you look like a million bucks this evening. I hope Lil' Mike knows what a woman he has."

Mary smiled and said, "He knows, Mama Lou and he certainly knows how to appreciate his woman."

Mary answered the door and Michael stepped in and grabbed her, not knowing that Mama Lou was there. When he finished kissing her like he was going to rip her clothes off right there in the living room, Mama Lou said, "And good evening to you, sir." Michael looked like a little boy caught with his hand in the cookie jar. He went over and gave Mama Lou a big hug.

"See, Mama, you understand why we should just go to the courthouse Monday morning and get married."

"And keep me from wearing my new dress! Forget it. That would be a killing offense. You just hold on; it won't be long. Now you two get out of here and I'm going home."

Mary locked up while Michael escorted Mama Lou to her door. When he met Mary on the sidewalk, he put his arm around her and said, "Angel, you were just saved by the bell. Come to think of it I was just saved from a royal chewing out by my dad for missing the Company Christmas gala. Hey, but there is a first time for everything. Right? Mary punched him playfully on the arm and they entered the limo.

When they got settled, Mary opened her bag and retrieved the necklace. She turned to Michael with the necklace. She kissed him and put it in his hands. She turned slightly so he could fasten it around her neck. When he secured it, he bent down and kissed the back of her neck. He kissed it around until he was facing her.

"Mary, you mean so much to me. I can hardly wait until we are married so that I can make love you and hold you and kiss you and I never have to stop. I will never have to sleep alone or lie in bed and toss and turn because you are not there.

"I thank you God, for giving me this woman to love. Thank you that she loves me too."

Mary kissed the palms of his hands and then reached up and lovingly stroked his face. "I love you Michael Scott. I love the man that you are, the gentle giant that you are. You deserve all the happiness that I can give you and I'm going to spend the rest of my life loving you and keeping a smile on your face 24-7."

They kissed and to them time stopped. They had no idea how long they had been kissing, but they noticed the car wasn't moving. Leon had stopped a few blocks away from the Hartford Marriott. Mary took her compact and began refreshing her face. Michael was busy wiping lipstick from his hands and face. After they inspected each other, the car pulled off and shortly, the smiling couple exited holding hands. Mary winked at the Leon and he smiled and winked back.

Chapter 13

December 17

Michael and Mary had been Christmas shopping together, which was eye opening for them. On the previous day, Michael went shopping with Mary. She bought gifts for the women in her Bible study group at the nursing home. She also purchased gifts for the Scotts, Mama Lou, Phillip, Leon, and both the housekeepers and the Scotts' cook. She bought gifts for her pastor and his family. For her closest friends at church she bought pretty items for their collections. One collected cups and the other two collected owls and elephants. Next, he helped her bake and package dozens of cookies for the nurses at the hospital, the library staff and the staff at the church and in the church book store.

Today, Michael bought gifts for his secretary, Deloris; Phillip; the office manager; his parents, Mama Lou, and the house staff. Gifts for Leon; his board members; his management team; his relatives far and near and their children finished his holiday shopping. Michael spent more money than Mary thought was necessary. He spent more than she had in a year! But it was his money. It was only money; he was used to spending it and he had millions to spend. She had to keep telling herself that it was not her concern. One day she was going to ask him how he kept up with how much he had. Michael knew that Mary was uncomfortable with his spending and wanted to try to help her understand.

A few evenings later, while they were sitting down in front of the fireplace in his home, he asked, "Mary, the way I spend money bothers you, doesn't it? It seems that I am careless and that I throw money away. Let me help you to understand. The money I have available to spend, the money in my checking account, is just the interest on the money I have actually earned. You don't ever have to worry about money or bills again. We have more than we could spend in a lifetime, even if we spent $15,000 a day! Do you understand angel?"

"Yes Michael I understand. That makes me feel better. I still can't wrap my mind around spending like you do, but trust me I can really appreciate not having to worry about bills ever again. Thank you, my love. Thank you, God. This knowledge will certainly keep your wife from having worry lines across her face because of financial worries. I am free to relax and enjoy my life. Now I'll worry about something else."

"Like what?" he asked.

"Oh, I don't know. Maybe I'll worry about when you're going to join Shiloh. Can you help me with that?"

Michael stood up and stretched. "I've been going to church with you."

He was right. He had told her he was going, and he had only missed this past Sunday. She knew he had a good heart and she knew he loved and trusted God. He just did not like to be associated with one church for some strange reason. But she knew that somehow, God would fix that situation in His own time.

"Where are you going?" Mary asked.

"To pop some popcorn. You want some?"

"Sure, and if I can't fit into my wedding gown you will be v-e-r-y sorry."

"Does that mean then you would have to come down the aisle naked?"

"Only in your dreams, giant." He laughed all the way to the kitchen.

Mary thought about the money Michael had; all the things she would love to see him do for people who needed so much, but who were so appreciative of the little things people did for them. If only she could show Michael that all he needed was to belong, be a part of a church family; be a part of a group of people who would show him love with no strings attached. Being a member of a church didn't keep you from visiting other churches. It just gave you a home; a place where you were a member of one of God's families. He just needed to experience that feeling of belonging; not like he was a person that people admired from afar or someone who saw him as a means to their selfish ends.

Michael could pray and sing just like every deacon in Shiloh. Truth be told, he could pray and certainly sing better than several of the men on the deacon board. All he needed was some male friends. He needed to meet some men who were comfortable in their own skin and who were not intimidated by another man, no matter how much money he had.

That was the solution to Michael's refusal to become a member of the church. She knew he read his Bible, because the one he carried to church was as worn as hers. He knew God. Now she was going to make sure he met some of God's Shiloh men. She was going to show him that he had some spiritual brothers on earth. She was going to start planning a get-together so they could meet. Michael was so humble and unpretentious that if you met him on the street, you would never know he was a multimillionaire.

Michael was pondering how to start a special holiday tradition that would be significant for him and Mary. He knew it would have to be something that didn't involve his money. Well, at least nothing elaborate. He thought about getting a group of people together to go caroling. They could have an early chili supper in his home and then leave and go caroling. Maybe he could rent a party bus. Then afterwards, they could come back to the house for gingerbread, to open gifts and drink some hot chocolate.

Who could he ask? The folks he knew he could ask would come just because he asked them. That was not what he wanted. He wanted people to come because they wanted to spread some holiday cheer and brighten this season for people who may not feel in the holiday mood; people who were not as blessed as he was. He wanted to bring it up to Mary, but he wasn't sure whether she thought it was old fashioned. The idea was growing on him and he kept adding things that the group could do. Have a holiday party at the nursing home. Maybe taking them to see the Christmas lights one evening in a party bus. What about letting some children from the library go ice skating and roasting hotdogs? Of course Santa would have to make an appearance.

He gave Mary the bowl of popcorn and he continued thinking about his caroling idea. His thoughts were interrupted when Mary asked, "Have you come up with any ideas of things we can do to start a Christmas tradition?" Michael hesitated and Mary knew he had something to say. He stretched out and put his head in her lap.

"What about getting a group of 10 or 15 people together to go caroling? We could do a tradition for the 12 days of Christmas." He explained and she listened. Then she got into the spirit of what he was thinking and before long they had more ideas than they had days. There was one thing for sure. The Scotts were certainly going to have some holiday traditions worth writing home about!

They had a list of things to do. But because of all the other things going on at the moment, they settled on two. The first one was to get a group together and go caroling on Christmas Eve. Mary would ask some of the men from church and Michael was going to ask some of the people at the office. They decided to limit it to 10 each. They would have a chili/chowder supper with all the trimmings.

They would visit as many places as they could. There were 18 nursing homes and they would go to as many as they could. They would not rehearse nor would they know who was coming until everyone got there.

Mary would make sure there were song sheets for everyone. The nursing homes would be contacted and given an approximate time to expect the group. Michael would have Deloris arrange the transportation and get a caterer. Afterwards, everyone would come back to the house for hot chocolate and surprise gifts from Michael and Mary.

Mary loved the idea. Once she began talking about it at church, others began to ask her if they could come. She ended up with 17 people and she was sure they probably would all show up. Michael was shocked when people started asking about joining the carolers. He ended up with 12!

They worked hard and when everything was ready, Michael was on cloud nine. He was going to love this tradition. Next year the gifts would say "From the Scotts". That brought a huge smile to his face.

CHAPTER 14

December 20

Tonight was the Pan Hellenic Council of Greater Hartford's Red and White Ball. Mary was really excited to be going. She had heard about it and seen the media coverage of this event in the newspapers for years. This was her first time attending. The sororities and fraternities were very active in the area and they did a lot of good things in the community. She never dreamed she would ever be attending this ball. Michael Scott, a past national officer of the Omega Psi Phi Fraternity being her escort, was over the top for her. She was both excited and nervous.

She was so glad she still had a new red dress to wear. She wondered if Michael bought that dress with this particular gala in mind. No doubt he did, being the ever efficient man that he was. Mary smiled when she thought about her giant.

He was working on the details of the Christmas caroling event and pulling out the stops. She had to keep reminding him to not overdo things; like giving all the women diamond studs and the men gold cuff links. They settled on cashmere scarves for the women and leather gloves for the men. Bless his heart, Michael just enjoyed giving and making people happy which made Mary adore him even more. Mary smiled when she thought about how excited Michael had become about the Christmas Caroling Chill/Chowder Supper.

However, everyone present at the ball this evening would not be smiling. No doubt there would be some women present who dated Michael at one time or another. But tonight and from now on, she would be on his arm and her engagement ring will tell the rest of the story. Since their engagement, there have been no pictures of Mary in the papers, so even though everyone knew Michael, very few people knew his fiancée. Tonight, she would be in the house! There would be no mistake about who Michael had chosen to become Mrs. Michael David Scott. Mary thought, 'I am so sorry ladies. But God made me for Michael and He made Michael for me; and yes, I really know I'm a very blessed and a truly loved woman. I'm a woman who is thankful for her blessings.'

Mary ate some soup and a sandwich and was relaxing with her tea when her phone rang. It was Mama Dot. They chatted a few minutes before she asked about the caroling. She didn't want to go with them she just didn't understand why they had not invited her. It took a minute, but Mary finally got her feathers unruffled. Then she wanted to know if they had any other plans that did not include her and Mr. Scott. Mary let her know that she would be included in any more plans they made during the holidays. Mary couldn't believe Michael hadn't asked his parents to join the carolers. She didn't think Mr. Scott cared one way or the other. This sounded like all Dorothy Scott. Mary didn't know why he had left them out but she was sure going to ask him.

Then she asked Mary about the New Year's dinner. Mary was going to host it at her house. It was going to be very intimate; just Mary and Michael, Mary's children and grandchildren and Mama Lou. Mrs. Scott wanted to know why she didn't have it at Michaels where there would be more room and she would also have more help. She tried to assure her that she had everything under control. But Mrs. Scott said she wanted Mary to feel a part of the Scott family which meant using everything at her disposal to make life easier. There was nothing Mary could say to get her to understand. She kept saying that she did not understand why Mary insisted on being all cramped up when it didn't have to be that way. Finally, Mary gave up. She could feel a headache coming on and she wanted to feel her best tonight. She gave in and agreed to have the New Year's Day dinner at Michael's. Mary knew she was feeling left out so she asked her about some serving dishes and she perked up. Mary promised to come over and get anything she needed.

The subject finally shifted and they began talking about the Red and White ball. Mama Dot reminisced about when she used to attend all the holiday galas. She admitted that they were just a bit too much for her now, and she would rather watch television while the television watched her. She said she wished she could see what Mary was wearing, so she told her if Michael came over early enough they would come by so she could see them on their way to the ball. She was satisfied said goodbye.

Mary was dressed when Michael arrived early, as usual. She didn't want them to be tempted to break their vow. When Michael saw Mary, he smiled and told her to turn around. She did and he took her in his arms and she could feel his hardness against her.

He trembled and Mary tried to move away. He held on and whispered in her ear, "You look amazing. You look delicious. I'd like to take that dress off and taste you all over. I'll give you $10,000 to stay home with me tonight and be my dinner."

Mary looked up at him and said, "No dice, buster, we're going to the ball."

He shook his head, kissed her on her forehead and as she picked up her coat and bag Michael stopped.

"Hold it" he said as he reached into his pocket and pulled out a jewelry box.

"Michael, you really don't have to do this. This dress doesn't need any extra jewelry, sweetheart." When she opened the box she was speechless. There was a pearl and diamond choker-style necklace and matching earrings.

He said, "May I put them on you?"

He put the necklace around her neck and it was absolutely perfect. Not too big, not too small but perfect. She removed her diamond studs he bought her last week and put on the pearl and diamond drops.

She reached up and ran her tongue over his lips and pulled him down to her. She whispered in his ear, "You are the most generous man on earth and I'm so glad you're mine. Very soon, I will give myself to you and we will make each other soar blissfully through the atmosphere. This, my giant, I promise you."

She kissed him and they both knew that it was definitely time to leave. She used the mirror in the entryway to redo her lipstick and Michael stood behind her fixing his face and adjusting his clothes. Mary thought it's a perfect place to have a mirror these days. Satisfied that they were presentable, Michael helped her slip on her coat and they walked out the door. Mary told Leon to take them by the Scotts. When Mary told Michael she promised his Mom they'd stop by he just smiled and said "I love you angel." She said, "I know, giant. We are a hopeless case."

They arrived at the Hyatt House Uncasville at the same time several other cars pulled up. Michael was greeted by two men and their ladies along with several unattached women exiting other cars. The women were looking at Mary harder than the men. Michael didn't bother to address anyone in particular, but he did say to those nearby, "May I present my beautiful fiancée and my future wife in 44 more days, Mary Elizabeth Cross. Come angel, let's get inside." He placed her hand over his arm and ushered her inside. All eyes followed them but none of their feet moved an inch.

Mary was in total shock. "Michael, what on earth was that all about?"

"I was just breaking the ice, angel. Just breaking the ice." he said and smiled as he kissed her on the cheek as her face broke into a smile that made his heart swell with pride.

There was a short line at the coat check counter. As they waited, Michael bent down near her ear and said, "If you're good to me later, I'll explain it."

"Exactly how nice do I have to be?" He winked at her and they laughed and Mary playfully hit him on the arm.

As quickly as they were shown to their seats, people began meandering, over to them causing Michael to stand up. As soon as introductions were made and a little small talk about the fraternity or the latest, hot political issue were mentioned, they would leave with a promise to be in touch. Michael would sit down and reach for Mary's hand and someone else would appear. This went on so long until they began to laugh about it. Michael wanted to leave and get drinks but he could never leave the table. They looked at each other wanting badly to make private comments but they didn't have a moment to themselves.

They were super elated when the band started playing. They escaped the barrage of well-wishers by quickly going to the dance floor. Mary went in to Michael's arms and he squeezed her for a brief moment and released her with a sigh that almost sounded like a groan.

"Did I tell you how astonishingly beautiful you look tonight?"

Her heart started to flutter and she looked up and smiled. She never knew quite what to say when he complimented her so sincerely.

She finally said, "I owe it all to my benefactor, my best friend, my giant and my soon to be husband and lover, whom I love very much."

He bent down and kissed her squarely on the lips. The room faded into the background as she put her hand on his chest and felt his heart beating wildly. The music stopped and they eased apart and floated to the refreshment table hand in hand. The parade to their table continued all evening. After about 3 hours, they couldn't take it any longer. Michael said their goodbye to the hosts and hostesses and wished them happy holidays. When they reached the car, Michael didn't wait for Leon to open the door. He held it open and followed Mary inside. As soon as they were settled, he took her hand and said how grateful he was to her for showing so much patience and understanding to all the curious folks tonight. She assured him that it was not a problem and that he should forget about it because the evening was over. He smiled at her and said, "Like hell. Not yet, it's not." They kissed quickly as the car headed to her house.

Michael told the Leon he could take off and he would call him tomorrow and give him the time for a Monday morning pick-up. The trunk opened and Michael took out a gym bag, a garment bag and his laptop and briefcase. He had Leon get back in the car and he walked up to the porch looking like he was going on a trip.

Mary unlocked the door and he walked right past her and went down the hall into his old room. When he came out, his tie was gone and so was his overcoat and tuxedo jacket. He kissed the top of her head as he passed her and went into the living room to make a fire.

Mary was so stunned she had barely moved away from the front door. When he finished the fire, he went into the kitchen and put the kettle on and got two mugs from the cabinet and looked up at her with a smile, "So are you going want chamomile or lemon berry?" She finally got over the shock of his boldness and replied, "Lemon-berry please. And if I might be so bold as to ask, what just happened here?"

He finished putting the mugs, teabags and honey on a tray and took them into the living room and sat down. She followed him out of the kitchen and stood in front of him, impatiently waiting for an explanation.

"I'm going to church with you in the morning right? So, I figured we could go in your car. So, no need to keep Leon on call the whole weekend. I know we can and we have safely slept in the same bed part of the night and that's what I want Mary. I can't leave you here and be alone tonight. I realize it will be tempting, but I also trust God enough to believe that He will allow me the pleasure of sleeping with you in my arms. Will this be allowable tonight?"

Mary hung her coat in the closet. "I suppose it will be alright." Mary answered, "I just hate for people to see us in the morning leaving the house together. It will look like we have been doing something wrong. I don't care what people think, but I do want to keep my reputation as a Christian women who is above reproach.

She went down the hall into her bedroom and began removing her jewelry and Michael came up behind her and kissed her on the neck. Mary froze and he laughed and unfastened the necklace and handed it to her. He unzipped her dress and neither of them moved. Within minutes, she heard the shower running.

She hung her dress and took a quick shower also. When she turned off the water, the kettle was sounding like a siren. She heard Michael open his bedroom door and go down the hall to the kitchen, and then there was silence. She dressed in some black and red lounging pajamas and matching house shoes.

They put the teabags into their mugs and snuggled on the sofa. Christmas music was playing softly and the man Mary loved was holding her in his arms. She couldn't be happier and she knew without a doubt Michael felt the same way.

"You know what? When we're married, we won't have sex every night. So this is just a test to see what that feels like." Michael said. "Who says we won't have sex every night? I'm healthy. Are you? What's to stop us?"

Michael fell back laughing and then he started tickling her. They laughed and played around enjoying the peace, the laughter and the love that surrounded them whenever they were together. They settled down drank their tea. After a few kisses they went to bed. They slept in Michael's room and they were both dreaming fantastic dreams very soon after they got in bed.

Sunday morning came too early. Neither of them wanted to get out of bed. They snuggled and kissed and whispered words of love to each other until 7:30 when the phone rang. The caller left a message and it was Mama Lou.

"Well good morning, you two. I don't suppose you are going to Sunday school Mary Elizabeth, so I'm going with Deacon Ellsworth. See you at the 11 o'clock service I guess." They looked at each other and busted out laughing. "You've got a great alarm clock, sweetheart." Mary said, "You better know it. But I wouldn't trade it for the world."

"What would you like for breakfast this morning? I've got...

Michael swallowed the rest of her reply with his lips. He ran his tongue around her lips and sucked on her bottom lip. He eased his tongue into her mouth and she sucked on it and his top lip. She moaned and he took her face between his hands.

She pulled away and her hands rubbed up and down his arms. His chest was damp. She bent and ran her tongue around his nipples. He tasted good and he felt wonderful. She feasted on his tiny nipple until he called her name.

She eased up and he captured her mouth in a burning kiss that made them both shutter.

"Let's get up before we do what we want to do." Michael said as Mary rolled over to keep him from seeing her tears.

"Beat you getting ready." And she jumped out of bed, and rushed across the hall to her room.

She hated not being able to satisfy Michael when she knew how badly he wanted her. She didn't know how many more cold showers they would have to take before they lost their minds. She sent up a petition to God as she prepared to dress for church.

CHAPTER 15

December 24

When Mary woke up and opened her eyes, the scene outside her window looked like a beautiful Christmas card. Fresh snow had fallen. Christmas Eve morning and Mary was excited as a child. She stretched and talked to God as she prepared for her day.

She was leaving for Michael's around 1pm. She wanted to make sure everything was going as planned. She dressed quickly and got into the car and that's when she saw the beautiful gifts she and Michael had wrapped the night before. She smiled as she thought about the fun they had and the future plans they talked about. She hoped everyone would like their gifts because she knew they would be completely surprised.

At Michael's she joined Mama Dot and Nellie, the cook, in the kitchen. They decided how the buffet would be set-up. Michael and Papa Jack were stacking wood and later, they arranged the gifts around the enormous Christmas tree.

Mama Dot and Mary came into the great room; both men stopped and looked up. Michael came to Mary and gave her a searing kiss while his parents enjoyed a long kiss themselves. Mr. Scott hugged Mary and she kissed him on the cheek.

They had a few minutes before the guests were to arrive so they took pictures and invited all the house staff to come in for pictures too.

Mrs. Scott presided over the gift giving to the staff. They opened their gifts and hugged and kissed the Scotts. Then Michael handed each person a card which Mary knew contained money. She didn't know how much, but based on the expressions on their faces, it was generous. They were all wished a Merry Christmas and told to go home and not to return until December 29th which was a BIG surprise to Mary and Mrs. Scott.

After they left, Michael decided to explain why he sent the staff home before anyone could ask.

"This is MY Caroling Party and it's an event that I am making an annual Christmas tradition starting this year. I think after all the staff has done already, I should be able to do whatever remains to be done. I should be able to serve as host to my guests, and if my almost wife will serve as hostess with me, everything will be truly perfect." Mary's heart skipped a beat and she smiled as Michael winked at her.

"The staff deserves to be with their family and friends on Christmas Eve. We have until December 29th to get the kitchen put back in order.

"Are you up for the challenge angel?" he asked coming toward her. She gave him a hug and a wink, "I think I can do my part, giant." The deal was sealed with a quick kiss.

Papa Jack walked over to the tree and picked up and passed out three gifts. He explained that this was a Christmas Eve gift and the Christmas gifts would be given after the caroling when everyone was gone. Michael opened his first, and was thrilled with his new cufflinks with diamonds surrounded by sapphires. They were beautiful. Michael hugged his dad. His wife ripped into her gift to find a chocolate diamond brooch and matching earrings. She was beyond thrilled and put the broach on her white sweater and left the room to look into a mirror. Mary held her breath while she opened her gift. She was speechless when she saw a beautiful diamond ring mounted in an heirloom filigree setting. She could only stare and Michael placed it on her right hand.

Papa Jack came over to her and wiped her tears.

"Mary, you have made my son happy and that makes me happy. This is to show you how happy I am to have you in our family. We love you Mary and thank you for making our lives complete, all three of us." Mary hugged Papa Jack and kissed him again.

"You and Mama Dot have filled a hole in my heart that I didn't even know was there. Thank you for accepting me and for loving me just the way I am. I love you both, and my life's mission is to assure this family of my love. It comes from God and His love never runs out. I promise you that my love is endless also."

She turned and gave Mama Dot a hug and kiss. The doorbell rang, and by the time everyone had composed themselves, Mama Lou was standing in the room with Leon who was loaded down with gifts. They rushed to her, hugging and kissing her as she made her way inside the house.

Michael had forgotten all about sending the car for her at 3:00. He was trying to remember whether he called and invited her over. He didn't have long to wonder because in her own grand style, she was ready to take over, even though she didn't know what was going on. After Papa Jack took her coat and purse, she sat down and beckoned for Michael who was helping Leon put the gifts under the tree. He came to her and knelt down so they were eye to eye.

"Now you listen here young man. I realize I don't have a lot going on in my life, but you could have called and ASKED me to be ready at 3:00 o'clock. It just so happened that when I saw Mary leave, I figured I'd better be ready for whatever God sent my way; so I got myself dressed.

"My presents have been wrapped for some time, so it wasn't a big deal to put them in a bag. But let me tell you something. You owe Leon a big tip for helping me gather my stuff and then waiting on me while I packed my bag. Oh yes! HE'S the one who insisted that I pack some things because HE knew I was expected to spend the holidays with the Scotts. Thanks, Lil Mike for checking with me first. I had not planned to go to the Bahamas this year for the holidays, so I didn't have to cancel any major plans. But, I DID have to call Mr. Collins. He invited me have Christmas dinner with him at Luby's, and I might add, he was very disappointed. See, what you made me do to my sweet gentleman friend; shame on you." She said as she hit Michael on his arm.

"Now, okay! I'm done fussing. I have worn myself out with all this rushing around and hustling and bustling." She looked up and said, "Now will someone please tell me exactly what's going on?"

Michael stood up and Mary reached for his hand while she and Mama Dot explained about the Chili/Chowder supper and the caroling plans. She was delighted and wanted to know what her duties were. Michael and Papa walked Leon to the door and gave him several gifts and cards. He assured them that Mama's bags were in her room in the cottage. He was off from work until the 29th and not only was he surprised, he had been kind of hoping to be in on the caroling. He hesitated and then said, "Mike, may I join the group for the caroling? If you don't have room for me in the bus, its okay; I can drive my own car. There's no one at my house and it's rather lonesome. I love to sing. I sing in the male chorus at Shiloh when I'm not working. I don't have to eat or anything, I just want to sing."

"Absolutely you can join us Leon. You are welcome to be our 1st guest of the day, after Mama Lou of course." The men laughed and Michael showed him a room where he could change and put his things. He retrieved his bag out of the limo and hurriedly changed and returned to the room where Mama Dot handed him a cup of hot chocolate. The doorbell rang and Michael popped Mary on the butt and said "Let's do this angel."

"I'm with you giant! Let's get this show on the road." Counting Mary and Michael and Leon, there were 32 carolers. The entire evening was fun for everyone and the host and hostess were simply over the moon!

After hugs and waves and Merry Christmas to James and Sadie, the house was finally quiet again. Mary and Michael had gathered up the last of the debris from all the presents and cleaned up the kitchen. It was 1:30 and they should have been exhausted, but they were still on a high from all the evening's activities.

The food was delicious, the gifts were appreciated and accepted for what they were, expressions of love from the hosts. The carols were beautiful and Leon surprised everyone by singing "White Christmas" for the group on the bus. A joyous time was certainly had by all and Papa Jack and his crew went home to share Christmas with not only Mama Lou, but Leon too!

Michael and Mary held hands as Michael went around turning out lights, extinguishing candles and locking the doors. They slowly made their way up the curving staircase, to the soft sounds of The Christmas Song coming from somewhere in the house.

Their thoughts of the many wonderful nights to come made them look at each other at the same time. They reached the bed and they fell across it with a burst of laughter. Neither of them thought of sex but instead, they thought of holding each other and drifting off to sleep as they had done several times. Mary moved first as she leaned over and kissed Michael on the forehead.

"I'll be back in a few."

"Don't be too long" Michael said as he stood and walked to his bathroom.

They both took quick showers. They got in bed and silently snuggled. Michael was hard and Mary hated to know that she couldn't satisfy his needs. She turned her back to him and he nestled his hardness against her.

"Merry Christmas, my angel. I love you so much. This has been the best Christmas Eve of my life" he whispered in her ear.

Mary didn't answer for a minute and Michael knew she was crying. She finally turned over and put her arms around his neck.

"Oh, my sweet giant. You continue to give me the happiest time of my life every day I am with you. You are the perfect example of what giving and Christmas are all about. I love you dearly Michael. I will never stop loving you."

They kissed and their tongues danced as their hearts beat to the same rhythm. Michael brought her closer to his hardness and she rotated her hips. He nuzzled her neck and the laid his head on her shoulder. He tried to move away from her, but she was relentless as she rubbed against him. Her breathing was coming in gasps and he abandoned his efforts to break away from her and held her tighter while she added more friction by pulling him over her and putting her legs around his back. Mary could feel the explosion building as she increased her efforts. Michael pulled her up and down against him and she stiffened. He groaned into her ear and they both reached that point where they floated through the clouds. He called out her name and she screamed his name and felt his release through her pajamas. Their movements slowed and they kissed as if it was a first kiss. Exploring and tasting each other.

Michael rolled onto his back bringing Mary with him. She relaxed her legs and sighed.

"Wow. You are some woman angel. How did you know I needed that release?"

She smiled while he looked up at her, planting soft kisses all over her face "Because I knew I needed a release, too, Michael. Remember, we are two sides to the same coin, we are just alike. The same thing that makes you happy makes me happy too."

He kissed each of her breasts and she playfully pushed him away. "Good night Michael Scott. Merry Christmas."

"Good night angel."

CHAPTER 16

December 25

Christmas was very untraditional this year for the Scotts and for Mary and Mama Lou, too. Michael had the traditional Christmas meal with all the trimmings catered and delivered to his parents' cottage on Christmas Eve morning. The meal would be served at 2pm. Michael and Mary enjoyed a relaxing breakfast and kept on their pajamas until it was time to go to lunch. Not getting dressed and being carefree without having to be somewhere that morning was a treat they both enjoyed tremendously.

They arrived at the cottage at 2pm and everything was ready. Mama Lou looked beautiful in her lovely black velvet pantsuit. Mama Dot wore a red velvet jacket with a Christmas plaid hostess gown.

Leon was there in a holiday sweater he received from Mary. They had insisted he invite his lady friend, Janice. He was touched by their generosity. She accepted his invitation and she was introduced to everyone and made to feel welcome. The sound of the doorbell signaled another guest, Mr. Collins. Mama Lou's friend had arrived. He too was welcomed and introduced to everyone and made to feel right at home among friends.

Mama Lou took his hand and walked him to a seat. Before he sat down, he pulled her into his arms and kissed her, to the surprise and delight of everyone.

Mama Lou blushed and said, "Alright Mr. Collins, now don't you go getting all frisky now."

Mr. Collins, reached in his pocket and gave her a gift and said, "Merry Christmas, Ruthie Louise." She sat down and opened the gift to find a tennis bracelet made out of her birthstone and diamonds. She smiled and had Janice to put it on her wrist. Everyone was happy for her. She smiled at Mr. Collins and said, "I'll give you yours later." Of course everyone took that and ran with it for the rest of the afternoon. Every time Mama Lou left the room, the remarks had to do with when she was going to get Mr. Collins' gift and what it might be. Everyone had fun teasing them and they enjoyed being the talk of the day.

The men sat in front of the fireplace talking about the playoffs and making sure they knew what time the Dallas-Washington game would be telecast. The women were putting the finishing touches on the meal. They called everyone to the table and Mr. Collins prayed. The meal had all the trimmings; everyone ate and enjoyed the lively dinner conversation and the good food.

Mary and Joyce cleared the dishes and Mrs. Scott served dessert. Not to be left out, Mama Lou insisted on serving the coffee. She didn't scald a single person or spill a drop. The dessert was a choice of apple pie and ice cream, pecan pie or berry cobbler. Everyone was finished just in time as the game came on. Leon, Janice and Mr. Collins were the only ones pulling for the Cowboys. At half time, the dishes were quickly loaded into the dishwasher and the food was put away. More dessert was served and sometime during the second half, everyone took a nap. When the game was over, gifts were exchanged and everyone was pleased with their gifts. Leon had to take Janice home and invited Mr. Collins and Mama Ruth to join them for the ride and they did.

The older Scotts sat on the sofa and snuggled while Michael and Mary sat on the love seat. Mama Dot thanked Michael for being thoughtful and ordering the food. She said she didn't remember ever feeling as relaxed after a Christmas meal. He smiled down at Mary and said it was her idea. You could feel the love and serenity in the room; everyone was relaxed. The peace of the holiday could certainly be felt in the quiet stillness of the Scotts' home. It was a beautiful day and Michael and Mary were silently thanking God for their love on His birthday.

The rest of the week was spent getting everything ready for the New Year. Removing the holiday decoration and packing it away at Michael's house was the biggest order of business. Mary had been going through her things, throwing away things she no longer needed, putting things aside to give to family and friends and separating and boxing up things going to Michael's. She also had a pile of things she had no idea what to do with.

She didn't want to put anything in storage so the entire ordeal was a very slow process. All three of her bedrooms looked a mess.

At the same time, she was slowly prepping foods for her New Year's Day dinner. It would be the first time she would prepare a meal for the Scotts and the first time she had cooked at Michael's. She wanted everything to be perfect but oddly, she wasn't nervous.

She had washed and cooked the chitterlings and the greens were washed early in the week. The greens were ready to be cooked, the corn was shucked, and the black-eyed peas shelled. She was quite busy and she loved it. Most of her usual activities were cancelled during the holidays so she had some extra time and she needed every bit of it. Everything would have to be boxed and transported to Michael's where some of it would be cooked.

Along with all of that, she was working with a caterer on the phone and trying to reason with Mama Dot about the menu for the wedding reception, which had somehow morphed from a simple buffet of cheeses, fruit and veggies to a full 4 course meal for 600 guests, an increase of 400 people. She was so grateful that because Mama Dot had insisted they have the invitation lists ready when they selected the invitations, Henri had taken care of addressing the envelopes. That was truly a blessing she almost had missed.

The cost for more centerpieces, table linens, chair covers and food servers went up through the roof. What had been an initial budget of $15,000 had passed $48,000 and was steady rising, almost daily. Invitations alone had increased from $9600 to $13,500 not including postage! She knew Michael didn't care, but it was still extremely extravagant to Mary and she didn't like the idea of the whole thing costing so much.

CHAPTER 17

·+·◆◆◆◆·+·

January 1

Mary and Mama Lou went to Watch Night service and afterwards prayed together at Mama Lou's before Mary went home. Michael wanted to come over, but Mary insisted that she had a lot to do when she got up and needed to get to sleep quickly. He understood and didn't try to convince her otherwise. He promised to see her early enough to help her do anything she needed him to do.

Mary was up New Year's morning before the sun. She had her day planned and she was working her plan much to her satisfaction when her phone rang. She answered and smiled when Michael said, "Good morning, beautiful. Happy New Year!" She would never get used to hearing her giant's titillating baritone voice.

"Good morning, and Happy New Year to you too, my handsome giant. How is everything going?"

He chuckled, "It will be better once I see you. What are you up to?"

Mary related her plans and where she was in that plan along with all the tasks that remained in order for her to get everything done that she had to do before transporting everything to his house.

"Listening to you, it doesn't seem like there is anything I can help you do. How about some company?" he asked, hoping she would say yes, although it was 13 hours before the 6 o'clock meal. She laughed and made him promise that he wouldn't get in her way. He promised and said good bye.

Just then the doorbell rang. She thought to herself, if these interruptions don't stop, she would never have things ready on time. She looked out and saw Michael and her heart did a double beat. She opened the door and Michael was standing there wearing a big smile and looking good enough to eat. He wore a beautiful brown tweed blazer, a white shirt and brown wool slacks carrying a bag and a bouquet of fragrant flowers. He came in and she popped him on the butt before she shut the door. He deposited the bag and flowers on the kitchen island and reached for her like a starving man in an all you can eat buffet. They kissed greedily and gasped for air when they finally separated. She moved around him and he tried to catch her but he missed.

He hung up his coat and returned to remove the contents of the bag. He had a tray of sliced tomatoes, sliced cucumbers, red onions, and green onions surrounding a bowl of chow chow. She looked at him questioningly and he answered before she could ask, "I just knew."

She came up to him and kissed him soundly on his lips, taking her tongue and slowly tracing his lips before latching on to his bottom lip that she sucked and licked while he greedily reciprocated until she felt her skin tingling as his hands lightly rubbed up and down her back. He had pulled her shirt out of her pants and she never felt a thing. She slowly stepped back and patted his chest.

"Stay out of my head, giant."

"Hey, it's the only thing of yours I *can* get into so don't begrudge me that." She smiled and shook her head; she told him to behave or she would call Mama Lou on him.

He reluctantly sat on one of the stools at the island. He lovingly watched as she continued glide around in the kitchen preparing the fresh corn, diced red, orange and green peppers for frying; eggs were boiled and cooling for deviled eggs; 3 different cheeses were grated for the macaroni and cheese; the roast was prepared and put in the oven. He watched her make a banana pudding and put the layers together of her beautiful carrot cake.

After she had everything prepared, boxed and bagged, she took a quick shower and dressed. She had decided to wear a hostess gown in beige, brown and orange African fabric. She asked Michael if he approved and his answer was to kiss her breath away. They vowed their love to each other.

Mary turned to go back into the kitchen but she stopped when Michael asked if he could see the color of her underwear. She hesitated for a moment. But she finally slowly lifted up the dress and revealed orange lace! He licked his lips and ran his hand over her mound. She backed away from him until she hit the wall; he took her mouth and gave her his tongue as his hand went inside her panties. She moaned and called his name. He worried her nub with his thumb and it was standing hard, hot and ready. He wanted it in his mouth but he knew he wouldn't stop if he did, so he slide two fingers into her hot, moist love tunnel and she trembled. He moved his fingers in and out quickly going deeper each time. She was holding on to him for dear life. She was about to make that tumble when he took one of her breast into his mouth, sucked and tongued her nipple until she called his name and ground her core onto his fingers. He swallowed her scream as her warm essence ran down his fingers. He put them into his mouth and they both licked them and continued kissing.

"You taste yummy, sweet angel. This is what I want for dessert tonight - angel sauce. Promise I can have it. Promise me?" "I promise, Michael." He bent and quickly licked the wetness from between her legs. He sucked her through her panties and she moaned. He was about to get a head start on his dessert, when the oven timer went off. He helped her sit down he went to get a towel. She wiped her legs and his face. Mary said, "We have to really wash our faces before we leave this house, Michael." He nodded, as he sucked his fingers holding the towel up to his nose as he headed for the bathroom. Mary went into her room, washed herself and changed her panties.

They returned to the dining room where everything was ready to be put in Michael's SUV. The flowers were brought for Mary's home, so they put them in a vase on the dining room table. Once everything was loaded, Mary checked the refrigerator one last time to make sure she had not forgotten anything. Sure that she had what she needed they headed to Michael's. She thought to herself, how in the world would she have gotten all this stuff in her car. Silently she said, 'God, I know you sent Michael and I certainly do thank you. Now please bless this food and all who will partake of it.'

At Michael's, the table was set for 22 and the center pieces were perfect. They unloaded the food and Mary went into the kitchen and began putting food in the ovens, and on the stove and in the refrigerator and on the counters. Food was everywhere.

Michael came in the kitchen, got a covered platter out of the butler's pantry and announced that these were oatmeal cookies; his contribution to the homemade desserts. He made them himself. Mary hugged and thanked him.

Michael continued to help, setting the desserts out on the buffet, and feeling quite pleased with himself. Mary was pleased with him too, in more ways than one! They couldn't be a more perfect couple and they knew it. Every time they passed each other they had to touch one another; it was as if they had to keep reassuring themselves that they were real and it was not a dream. The only thing left to do was make the hot water cornbread which would be done when the guest arrived so it would be hot when they sat down to eat.

The only people missing from this holiday meal this time were Leon and Janice. They were spending the time with her family in New York. So, Michael invited Phillip and his date. There were about 4 hours before the guests would start arriving, so they went into the bedroom and each got a quick sample of the dessert they both anticipated after dinner. They cleaned up and straightened the bed just as the doorbell sounded announcing the arrival of the first guest. Karen, Alford and Beverly and their families were all standing at the door. Michael greeted Alford with a man hug. Alford introduced his sisters and their spouses to Michael and he greeted the men with handshakes and the ladies with kisses on the cheek. He shook hands with all the grand children as they introduced themselves. Coming up the steps was Mr. Collins with Mama Lou on his arm. The housekeepers were taking the coats when Mary came in with her arms outstretched. The grand children were the first to grab her. She hugged and kissed them and then waited for her children who were talking with Michael. Mary asked the grand children if they would like to pass the time in the game room and there was a resounding yes. She asked Michael to show the kids to the game room.

Mary took the pound cake Mama Lou brought and sat it on the end table. She stood anxiously waiting for her daughters. They came to her along with their husbands. Through their tears the girls whispered how happy they were for her and how sorry they were for doubting her. She wiped away their tears and hers on her apron. Beverly spoke first, "Mama, we can see that you're happy and that's all we wanted. Just to make sure that you were happy."

Michael had walked up and put his arm around Mary, kissed her temple and said, "Hey, no fair hogging the cook." They all laughed and went into the family room to see if Mama Lou remembered who they were, and of course, she knew exactly who they were and she got all the names right.

Everybody was hugging laughing and talking when more guests arrived; Phillip and his date. The last to arrive were Michael's parents. He showed them in, hung up their coats and turned around. That's when everybody broke out laughing. He couldn't figure out the joke. At last, Mary walked up and wiped the lipstick off his mouth and untied his apron. He joined the laughter himself. His parents had never seen him in an apron and were so tickled they made him laugh at himself.

Everyone was called to the table shortly. Papa Jack said the grace. Then Michael said grace while holding Mary's hand. He thanked God for his new family and he prayed that the love in the room would remain in the family forever. When he finished, Andre' asked, "Anybody else want to pray? Lead a hymn maybe?" Everyone laughed. His mother said, "Watch it boy, or you won't get to eat." Karla said. "Maybe he wants to get banned from the table so he can eat in the kitchen where the food is coming from." His twin Andrea said, "Please don't put him in the kitchen or the food will stop coming because he will eat it all by himself." Everyone was laughing and the jokes and antics of Mary's grandchildren continued throughout the meal.

The entire meal was simply amazing. Papa Jack asked whether Mary had ever thought about catering and she answered no. Too much work and she only liked to cook what she liked. She wasn't into following the latest food craze and trying to prepare food from a lot of different countries.

Michael figured he had to say something, "Dad, she's already so busy she hardly has time for me. No way would I let her go into business." Mary smiled and said, "Excuse me, Michael." She paused, for effect, "Papa Jack, as I said, I don't think I want to expend the kind of energy it would take to cook for a large crowd of people every day. However, it is nice to know that you think I could make money selling my food. I didn't know it was above ordinary."

Her family and everyone at the table complimented her again and Michael got the picture. She had let him know that she had a mind of her own and she did it without even raising her voice.

When they finished eating, Beverly and Karen along with Phillip's date cleared the table and helped get everything back in the kitchen. Michael gave Mary's family a tour of his home while Phillip, Mr. Collins and Papa Jack talked about the football playoffs. After the tour, Mary's children had the longest drive, so they were the first to leave. Mary had take-out containers for everyone and she helped them make plates to go. Everyone took enough food home for probably two meals.

After the long goodbyes from Mary's children and grandchildren, their other guests began leaving also. The Scotts stayed a while and they talked about the wedding and reception. When they left, the door was shut and locked for the final time. Mary went into Michael's arms like they had been apart for months. "Are you too full for your dessert, Michael?". He growled his response. "I suppose not." Mary smiled as she removed her dress. She turned for him to unhook her bra. She removed his belt while he was unbuttoning his shirt. They fell onto the sofa and made love to each other the only way they could; each one giving as much love as each was receiving. Mary tumbled into the clouds as soon as Michael began to manipulate and suck on her breasts.

After Michael took her to his bedroom they continued loving each other until they climaxed together screaming each other's name. They kissed and got under the cover. They tumbled into their own special place in the clouds where millions of stars shattered into colorful starbursts. Mary finally stopped trembling and Michael kissed her wet swollen lips. They both said 'umm, umm, umm'. Mary scooted closer so she could feel his heartbeat against her ear. It always amazed her how their hearts beat the same rhythm. Michael held her gently, thinking how she was a perfect fit. They drifted off to sleep without saying a word. Words were not necessary. They had communicated everything that needed to be said on a very basic level.

The next morning after they showered, dressed and had breakfast, they took a thermos of coffee along with some bread crumbs and walked to a nearby park. The talked very little, but they held hands constantly and glanced at each other often.

They were thinking how blessed they were to have each other. They wanted to be married right now and time seemed to be stopped. They contemplated staying away from each other except on the weekends, but knew the other wouldn't go for it. So they sat quietly keeping their thoughts to themselves.

Michael left shortly after they returned to the house. He had to make some calls and follow-up on some things happening overseas. When he returned he took her home. He thanked her for letting him bring in the beautiful New Year in such an awesome way. They kissed good bye and he left.

The next weeks went by rather quickly. Mary saw Michael about 2 or 3 times a week. He had accompanied Mary and Mama Lou to church every Sunday for the past 4 weeks and she was thrilled about that. He was getting more and more comfortable at Shiloh. The men and women who went caroling with him made him feel like an old friend. No one acted like he was a multimillionaire. He was just Michael Scott, the fellow engaged to Mary Cross. He seemed to genuinely enjoy the sermons.

One afternoon while they were on the phone Mary asked, "Michael, what's bothering you? I know you're happy, but you are also unhappy about something and I can't figure out what it is. Is there anything I can do to make it better?"

He sighed and then he said, "I can't put my finger on it, but something is going to happen and it won't be good."

Mary questioned him and he couldn't say when he started feeling like something was amiss, but he knew something was about to change their lives. Mary told him to try not to think about it. She reminded him that sometimes the enemy will throw something bad into the mix just to change the happiness into sadness. He thanked her for the reminder and promised not worry about something that had not happened and may not happen. They ended the call promising to go out for lunch Saturday, and they promised to visit with the top two wedding photographers so they could make a final decision and select one of them to shoot their wedding photos.

CHAPTER 18

January 31

Saturday morning Mama Lou called Mary to come over and when she got there Mary was shocked. Mama Lou was sitting on the chair in her bedroom looking disheveled and not at all like herself. Mary rushed to her and touched her face which was burning up. She got the thermometer and checked her temperature. It was 103. She asked her what she had eaten and she said she hadn't for a day or so.

She picked up Mama Lou's phone and called 911. She took her cell phone out of her pocket and called Michael. He was there just before the paramedics loaded Mama Lou on the stretcher. He told Mary to get her coat and change her shoes and she could ride with him to the hospital. She got all of Mama Lou's papers and medications, locked the house and rushed to her house. She put on her shoes, got her purse and keys, and the matching jacket to the velour pants she had on. She locked her house and they were off to University of Connecticut Medical Center.

Mary knew that Michael was thinking that this was the premonition he had. She kept praying 'God, please don't take her now. Please, God, not now.'

Mary went to admissions and got Mama Lou admitted. She met Michael in the Emergency Room waiting area. Shortly after they sat down, the Scotts and Leon came in. Mary immediately went to Papa Jack first, then Mama Dot. Leon just nodded and stood by Michael. After a while, everyone settled down and waited for some word from the doctor. About 90 minutes later, they called for the family of Ruthie Thompson. The group stood and they were ushered into a smaller waiting room.

The doctor proceeded to tell them that Mama Lou did not have a stroke. Her condition was caused because she was dehydrated, and her pacemaker needed to be replaced. The dehydration made her mentally disoriented and it also caused the fever. She had not maintained the phone monitoring schedule from her cardiologist. If she had, the batteries in her pacemaker would have been checked and the doctor would have known when they needed replacing. She was admitted to the hospital so they could get her rehydrated and get her pacemaker replaced. She would be in the hospital two or three days, and barring any complications she would be good as new. They all thanked the doctor. He informed them that as soon as she was put in her room they could all visit.

Michael asked how to get her a private suite and the doctor sent him to admissions. Mary wanted to stop him, but she knew it was not the right time to try to tell him that in a semi private room she would have a roommate and that she would enjoy the company. Michael was all about her comfort and wanting her to have the best care and accommodations possible. She wouldn't dare try to stop that giant when it came to the people he loved. He had taken the admission papers from Mary and strode out of the room like he was the doctor in charge. When he returned, he was much more relaxed. He even smiled.

He announced that they preferred her in a semi private room so she would have someone to talk to. He knew how important talking was to Mama Lou and he agreed right away with the admissions clerk. About 30 minutes later a nurse told them that they could go to Mama Lou's room. They all got up and headed for the elevator. When they got to her room and opened her door, Mama Lou asked, "Did anyone think to call Mr. Collins for me?"

When no one answered, she said, "Well aren't you a loving family. Will one of you please call him and let him know my room number; his number is 743-2427. In case he needs a ride, his address is 10600 West High Pointe, High Pointe Apartments #208."

Leon spoke up, "I'll get in touch with him, Mama Lou."

"Thank you Leon. You're a good man."

"Now you Scotts listen to me carefully. I'm only going to be here long enough for them to replenish my fluids and to give me a new pacemaker. So you can relax. I'm not leaving this earth before I get to wear my dress in the wedding. Now is that clear?"

Everyone laughed and assured her that they couldn't think of anyone else standing in as the matron of honor. Michael and Mary kissed her on opposite sides of her face and told her they would be back later that evening to check on her.

Mama Dot was holding her hand when Leon came over and kissed her other hand. Leon left and Papa Jack walked Michael and Mary to the elevator. He shared some thoughts he and his wife had been discussing. They wanted to ask her to move into the cottage with them. They had a special suite on the ground floor that just happened to be empty and unused. It would be perfect for her and she would have privacy, but she wouldn't have to be alone.

Since Mary would be moving soon, it was the ideal thing for her to do. He wanted to know their thoughts. Michael confessed that he and Mary had also been wondering who would look in on her once Mary left. They had never thought about the elder Scotts. Mary hugged Papa Jack and Michael said if she would agree, they could have her all moved by the time she got out of the hospital and it would be a lot easier for everyone. Papa Jack promised to take a shot at talking to her about it and he would call when he got her answer.

Michael and Mary headed to meet the first photographer with lighter hearts and a future that looked even brighter. Their meeting with the second photographer left them even more torn between the two, so they agreed to hire them both. There would be enough opportunities for both of them to showcase their photography genus by capturing sweet moments of their everlasting love.

Papa Jack called; Mama Lou agreed to move and was very happy that she would still be close to Mary, who would be in the "big house" which is what she called Michael's house. Michael's house had 8 bedrooms and 9 1/2 bathrooms. The "Cottage" had two bedroom suite with its separate living and dining space, and the remaining part of the cottage had 4 bedrooms and 4 baths.

The hospital had agreed to keep Mama Lou until that Wednesday. That meant they had 4 days to get her things packed, moved and unpacked.

They hurried to Mama Lou's and started making calls. Mary called Lois Jones and Billie Fisher, her two friends from church. She knew they would help and would be discreet with whatever they saw in Mama Lou's home.

Michael called his housekeeper Josie and asked her to have Martha, the Scotts' housekeeper get the suite in the cottage prepared for Mama Lou.

He called Phillip to get a moving company to pick up her things. He wanted him to order some boxes and wrapping materials to be delivered today for Mary and Mama Lou. The packing boxes and packing material arrived as they were finishing up their late lunch. Lois and Billie were coming up the sidewalk as the men were putting the boxes in her house.

Michael and the women started in the dining room; they packed china, linen, crystal and silver. Michael put the boxes together and moved them as they were filled. They made quick work of the first room and moved into the living room. They took down the pictures, packed books, picture albums, "dust collectors" and ash trays of every description; the drawers in the end tables and coffee table were emptied onto newspaper on the floor; Mary saved them in a trash bag for Mama Lou to go through when she got settled.

The doilies, and cushion covers were put in a bag to be laundered. Michael decided the furniture was not worth moving. However, the ladies knew she would want her doilies on whatever furniture she had in her new home.

The bathroom and the hall closet were easy to empty, as was the guest bedroom. The linen was removed to be laundered. The bedroom furniture was antique and valuable but there would not be any place for it in the suite. Michael decided to have them to bring it and they would find somewhere to put it between his house and the cottage. The mattress was to be thrown out along with the pillows and box springs. When they moved the mattress there was a garment bag underneath it. Michael picked it up and they all wondered what was in it. Michael laid it on the box springs and they got the surprise of their lives! They found money rolled up with rubber bands. They were shocked, to put it mildly. Mary opened a roll and counted $200 dollars; there were 68 rolls so there was potentially $13,600 in the bag! They found a box of rubber bands and Mary bundled the money she had counted and put it back in the bag. Needless to say, that ended the work for the day. They agreed to return the next day after church so they could finish the last room, her bedroom, which was going to be the hardest room to pack up.

Mary locked the house and she and Michael walked the short distance to her house. Because Michael had not brought his clothes for church they decided that he could pick Mary up in the morning and he wouldn't have to drive back over to her house because it was getting late, and she knew he was tired. So was she.

He didn't like the idea of them not sleeping together. It had been weeks since they had slept together all night. He was horny and was looking forward to holding his angel all night. Mary tried to console him by reminding him they were only 14 days away from becoming husband and wife. Michael was not consoled and he left pouting like a child. Mary knew he would be okay and she also knew how he felt.

Michael arrived promptly at Mary's house. They left shortly for Shiloh where the service was spirit-filled and many lives were changed. Michael became a member of Shiloh that day which surprised Mary because he had not said a word about his decision. She was thrilled as were the many friends and well-wishers at the church.

The Overtons invited them home for dinner and they accepted. They were one of the couples who went caroling and Michael and James seemed to really enjoy each other's company. He was a middle school principal and his wife Sadie ran a day care center. They enjoyed lively conversation and some really good food. Mary knew she and Michael had to go. They shared what they were doing about Mama Ruth's new living arrangement. The Overtons loved the idea and offered to help. Michael was glad for the company, and Mary knew she could use one more hand for the bedroom and kitchen. They agreed to meet at 4pm.

With the extra help things went quickly and a little before 11pm the house was ready to be emptied. Everyone was tired but happy that the house was all packed up. They had found another garment bag of money under the mattress in her room which contained approximately $24,000 in cash. Michael put the garment bags in a box and labeled it 'Mama Lou'. It was stacked with the others marked and ready for placement in the cottage. Mary thanked their friends for helping and everyone left.

Michael knew that Mary wanted them to refrain from anything other than light kissing until after the wedding; he knew she would not let him spend the night. He wasn't even allowed to put his hands on her other than on her arms. He was so frustrated, and it seemed to him that she was always doing something or wearing something just to give him an erection.

He could hardly wait to make her his in every sense of the word. Mary, on the other hand was thinking If Michael looked at her one more time with his eyes telegraphing his hunger for her, she was going to lie down wherever they were and just give in to him. She was having a really hard time keeping her panties dry. She changed panties sometimes three times in a day when he was around. He had no idea how much she wanted him. She was sleeping with the light on to keep from closing her eyes and reliving those passionate times they had shared. It was rough on both of them and they were on the edge of sanity with aching need for real physical intimacy.

CHAPTER 19

+ ◆ ◆ ◆ ◆ +

February 2

Mary met the movers next door at 8 o'clock; she directed them to the boxes going to the cottage; she decided against sending the money box so she had it taken to her house. Later that day, the Salvation Army came along with Goodwill and picked up items being donated. The better pieces of furniture were taken to the cottage and would fit perfectly in her suite. Mary had no idea about the dining room set, so it was also taken to the cottage.

Now she needed to select some living room furniture so it could be delivered and be in place when Mama Lou got to her new home. Mary wished Mama Lou was able to go and help select what she wanted herself, but she knew how long it took Mama Lou to make up her mind, so she nervously went alone with lots of uncertainty.

Mary knew what Mama Lou liked but these were very big decisions she was to making and she was anxious. She found the perfect living room set and before she started second guessing herself, she purchased it right away, along with window treatments, lamps, and end tables for the living room. She bought a mattress set, and a recliner for her bedroom, new bathroom accessories and matching towels; new bed linens and window treatments for the bedroom.

Mary knew Mama Lou liked to watch television; therefore, and she got her a 42 inch flat screen for the living room and a 37 inch flat screen to be mounted on the wall in the bedroom.

She was happy with her purchases and called Michael to tell him the progress she had made. He wasn't available so she continued on her mission for the day. She went home and cleaned her guest room and emptied the drawers, closet and bathroom. She swept, mopped, cleaned the mirrors and polished the furniture. She was tired and decided to quit. It was almost 8pm and she hated to think about cooking something for dinner. Her doorbell rang and before she got to the door, Michael said, "Hurry up woman, the food's getting cold!" She broke into a smile and thanked God for her loving, thoughtful giant.

"Michael! Do you have cameras in here? Is there a brain transmitter in my head connected to your brain? I was just thinking about how hungry I was and how I had no idea what to do for dinner."

He had put the food on the island and draped his coat over a chair; he took her in his arms and just held her; his erection poking her in the stomach. "You have no idea how much I have missed having you in my arms; no idea at all. Kiss me, Mary". And kiss him she did!

She held on as he plundered her mouth, tongues dueling, and moans of delight filling the room. Slowly, they pulled away from each other and smiled.

"I love you, my handsome giant. I love how you love and care for me. I can hardly wait to give myself to you completely because I am truly yours."

Michael took her left hand and kissed her ring, "You have made my life so complete until when you are not near me, I feel off kilter. I love you, my angel. I cannot imagine not having you in my life. I am yours and you, Mary Elizabeth, are my angel from God Himself. I will devote my whole life to keeping you happy."

Mary said, "I have no doubt that you will. Now let's eat; I'm starved."

"So am I" he responded.

They ate barbequed ribs, potato salad, baked beans, and garlic bread. He bought marble cake for dessert. They ate and talked. She talked about her purchases. They discussed their plans for the next day related to getting the houses empty plus getting Mama's things unpacked at the cottage.

Mary knew she was going to sale her own house including the furniture, so she didn't have a lot to move, but to her, it didn't seem like she had made a dent in her 'to do list'.

They agreed she should just work on Mama Lou's and just move her clothes. The things in her own house could be dealt with after they returned from their honeymoon. Mary was relieved with that decision made and she thanked Michael for making the decision.

They discussed ideas for their wedding photos and places they wanted as the background shots and what they would wear. They had appointments with the photographers next week to get started. Everything was under control, and if they could maintain that same control over their physical desires for eleven more days, they would be able to finally have that physical release they needed.

Michael complimented Mary on how well she kept up with the receipts and how she was so conscientious with her spending. He expressed his concern over her stressing herself out trying to find the best deals on everything. He reminded her that time was not a luxury; and, when she saw something she wanted to go ahead and get it.

They cleaned up after their meal and prepared to say good night. They held on to each other and it seemed like the whole world stopped as they lovingly kissed and held each other close. Mary stood in the door as Michael drove away with tears streaming down her face. She was so happy and so thankful for this man God had given her who loved her so much and showed it in everything he thoughtfully did for her.

The next day was cold and brisk as she prepared to meet the delivery truck at the cottage with her purchases from the day before. It arrived on time and the men placed the furniture and mattresses as instructed and removed the cartons and wrapping materials. She got some unexpected and very much appreciated help from Mama Dot and Martha, plus Josie from Michael's house.

They worked together like a well-organized team and quickly arranged everything and made the bed and set up the bathroom. Just as they completed the job, the moving truck arrived with Mama Lou's belongings from her house. Because the truck was late, the men quickly put the boxes from Mama's house into her new suite in record time. Now the process of unpacking and arranging began anew.

They stopped for a quick lunch of delicious Clam Chowder Nellie made for them. They continued working into the evening. They didn't stop until it was all done. They finished around 7pm and they were all tired as hell, but pleased with what they had gotten accomplished.

The suite was cute and looked just like something Mama Lou would have bought if she had spent the money Michael had spent. Papa Jack and Michael came in just as Martha was getting her things to leave for the day. They met Josie walking back up to the house to get her things and head home.

The men stood and gawked with their mouths open in shock. The empty suite had been transformed into lovely living quarters perfect for Mama Lou. It looked like a professional designer had been hired and that's what Michael asked. Mary was delighted that everyone liked what she had purchased and how everything had turned out. They all thought it was done by a professional. She prayed that Mama Lou would like it too. Everyone reassured her that she would love it.

Mary was so tired that she was about ready to pass out. She said her goodbyes, gathered her things to leave and Michael walked her out. He could see that she was utterly exhausted and it showed with every step she took. She didn't look like she had enough energy to make it to her car. Michael suggested she stay at his house and leave in the morning and for once, she didn't argue with him. They went into the house and he quickly prepared her a fragrant bubble bath which she truly appreciated.

She reclined in the jetted tub and soaked until Michael came in to check on her. She got out, dried off and came into the kitchen wearing one of Michael's t-shirts that came down past her knees. She gave Michael a hug and a kiss and he quickly gave her a turkey sandwich, chips and some champagne. He had eaten earlier so he had champagne and some chocolate cake.

They said good night following a long, sweet kiss. Michael rubbed his hands over her butt and he could tell Mary wasn't interested so he stopped. He led her to one of the guest rooms and tucked her in bed with a kiss on the forehead. She closed her eyes and very quickly sleep came, without dreams.

CHAPTER 20

February 4

Mama Lou was getting out of the hospital today and Mary was going to bring her to her new home. She was anxious and woke very early. She planned to leave a note for Michael but she was in for a big surprise. She thought Michael had asked Nellie to make breakfast for them but he was making breakfast. She felt truly loved.

He greeted her with a big smile and "Good morning, beautiful angel." She stopped in her tracks put her hands on her hips and asked, "Do you cook breakfast every morning?"

"No, only when I have my beautiful angel sleeping down the hall from me all night. I couldn't sleep soundly, so it was a no brainer to make your breakfast. I hope you're hungry." She picked up a piece of crisp bacon and promptly sat down at the breakfast bar. They enjoyed a breakfast of waffles, bacon and eggs.

Michael wanted to be with Mary when she picked up Mama Lou. After all, she agreed to move in with the Scotts, but she had no idea that someone else would go through her things, throw away and otherwise take charge of her belongings. If there was going to be any fall-out, he was going to take it himself. His aim was protect Mary in case things got out of hand. He had to go into the office first, and they decided that when he was finished, he would pick her up at her house. Together they would go to the hospital for Mama Lou.

They left Mary's at 11:15 and the drive was quiet. He knew she was worried about Mama's reaction to all that had been done without her input.

They were praying that Mama Lou would be pleased with what had been done for her.

When they got to her room, she was dressed and sitting in the wheelchair waiting for them. She fussed because they hadn't been to see her since they put her in the hospital. But in her heart she knew they were just a few days from their wedding and they had probably been very busy with wedding preparations.

They met with the discharge doctor who told them she was fine and as healthy as a horse. She needed to drink more water and have her pacemaker monitored every month. Someone would call from her cardiologist's office with specific instructions on the pacemaker monitoring. He kissed Mama Lou on the cheek and told her to behave. All the staff on her floor waved goodbye. They had to use three two-tiered carts to take all of her flowers and plants out of her room.

Michael was glad he brought the SUV and not the sedan. Mary got Mama Lou settled and they headed to Michael's. Of course, she wanted to go by home to get some more clothes. They explained that there wasn't any room to put anything else. They wanted to empty the car first.

The Scotts were standing out front of the cottage when she got out of the car. They hugged and kissed each other and oddly enough, she didn't fuss at them. Probably because they had been to see her while she was in the hospital. Papa Jack went every day. They wanted to show her the space they were thinking about for her.

When she stepped inside, everyone was holding their breath. She noticed her doilies and the new sofa and all the new stuff, but she kept seeing some of her things. She turned around and said, "Did I get moved in already?" But, before anyone could answer, she began to walk around and look at things and pick up pictures and open drawers and she put her hands on her hips and said, "Well, whoever did all this did a fabulous job. I love my new place. It looks just like in the magazines. It's beautiful; absolutely perfect."

Everyone cheered and clapped. Mary was so relieved, she felt a tear roll down her cheek and she didn't even know she was crying. Michael told her Mary selected everything and packed up her house and she was in charge of the whole thing. Mary was quick to tell her all the help she had; Lois, Billie, Sadie and James Overton, along with Mama Dot, Martha and Josie.

"Who do I owe for all of this?" she asked looking from one to the other.

Michael spoke up and said, "It's my gift to you for agreeing to be in my wedding. You don't owe me anything. Call it a payment for all the cookies you made in Georgia."

He hugged her and she wiped her eyes on the hankie she always had somewhere on her body. Mary and Mama Dot showed her to the bedroom and she was delighted, especially when she saw the wall mounted television. She loved the new recliner; she loved the bathroom and the walk-in tub the Scotts had put in the cottage last year.

Mama Lou said she just wanted to put on some clean clothes. Mary opened the closet and she had to sit down. That's when she knew she was really home. She saw all her clothes and shoe boxes and hat boxes neatly lined up on the closet shelf.

She stood up and hugged Mary and they rocked back and forth shedding tears of joy. Mama Dot eased out of the room. They had a moment to really let the water works flow. Both of the women knew without a shadow of a doubt how truly good God had been to them. They rejoiced and thanked the Lord as if no one was in the house but them. They would still live within shouting and walking distance from each other and that pleased them tremendously. They loved each other like mother and daughter and they were just as close as any mother and daughter could ever be.

After Mama Lou sat back down, Mary leaned over and said in her ear. "Did you forget about the garment bags of money under your mattresses?"

She gave a hardy laugh and said no, she hadn't forgotten the money. She said she bet they were shocked when they found it. They talked about it briefly and Mary told her it was boxed up at her house. She said "Keep it. I'll tell you how I got it one day," and that was the end of the discussion.

Mary showed her where her things were and left her to change clothes. For the homecoming celebration lunch, they had fried chicken, smashed garlic potatoes, mixed veggies, corn pudding and broccoli casserole. For dessert they had German chocolate cake. That was the first time in a long time both of the Scott men were home for lunch. Everyone had a great time and the food was wonderful. Papa Jack headed back to his office and Mama Dot rode with him since she had a fitting downtown near the office. Mary was going home to do a little more packing before she went shopping. Mama wanted to investigate her new home and had talked to Papa Jack about helping her plant some flowers. Michael was making arrangements for the honeymoon.

Everything in the world looked level again. Michael took Mary home and when he got inside her house, he asked for his credit cards. Mary was embarrassed because he should not have had to ask her for them. She had not thought about them since she finished buying the things for Mama Lou's new home.

She began apologizing for inconveniencing him and Michael cut her off.

"I want them back because you have your own cards. You won't need to have a letter to use them. Stop apologizing Mary, they are not the only cards I have. It was not an inconvenience. I love you angel, you don't ever need to apologize to me. Okay?"

She was one emotional lady and the tears started all over again. She walked away from Michael and tried to praise the Lord quietly, but she let it out and expressed her love for her Savior; she just kept thanking the Lord and calling Him by His many names.

Michael was touched and fascinated at the same time. He had seen her praise God in church, but he had no idea that she would do it at home. He had heard her with Mama Lou earlier.

He prayed silently while she got softer and quieter, "Lord, I want to know You and love You like Mary. I don't want to be ashamed or worry about what others may think. I want to experience You in my life and know that I can let go and let You run my life. Amen."

When he opened his eyes, with her face glowing and wet from tears of joy, Mary took Michael's hands and kissed the palms,

"One day soon, you will know the joy that comes from God. We'll study His word together. The more you know Him, the more you will love Him. After a while, your joy will overflow like mine and nobody will be able to stop you because you are a passionate man and God made you to praise Him. One day, giant, I promise. It will come." They hugged and Michael knew that the Holy Spirit was in the room. She gave Michael his credit cards and he gave her the replacements with her name on them, Mary E. Scott. They kissed quickly and Michael left.

Mary had done everything but get Mama Lou's phone service switched which she did immediately. She also had all the utilities turned off. She decided to go get Mama Lou and take her shopping with her. She knew they would both have fun. This was going to be an outstanding day, 10 days from her wedding day.

CHAPTER 21

February 8

When Michael picked up Mary for church, he had Mama Lou already in the car. She looked like a doll with her new tan suit and brown and tan hat with a sassy feather, brown low heels and matching bag. Mr. Collins was waiting for her when they pulled up. He stepped to the car and offered his arm. She stepped up to him and didn't look back. Michael and Mary smiled and went inside. He was so handsome in his dark blue suit with his blue and white shirt and yellow and blue print tie. He looked down at Mary and winked and she blushed from head to toe.

He said to her, "You look delicious this morning, angel. Rose is a good color on you." Mary wore a rose flair dress with a matching coat, black pumps and matching bag. Her jewelry was the diamond drop necklace and matching earrings Michael had given her.

After church, Mama Lou and Mr. Collins went to Park Place Cafeteria with some friends from his apartment complex. He said he would bring her home later.

So, being on our own, they didn't want to go home and be tempted so they headed to their favorite steak house. Just as they got to the door, Mary stopped suddenly. Something didn't feel right. Her mind said *"Go home. Do Not Enter. Eat lunch at home."* Mary had a premonition, while standing on the porch as Michael was about to open the door. She told Michael she changed my mind.

"I don't want to eat here today." He looked puzzled but he let the door close and they walked back to the car. She suggested they get a couple of steaks and she could rustle up a meal about as fast they could get served in the restaurant. He agreed and they headed for the nearest grocery store. Mary selected the meat while Michael got two potatoes; she had everything else at home.

Mike had a jogging suit in his gym bag so he changed his clothes. Mary changed and within the hour, they were sitting down to a wonderful meal. Mike's phone rang and it was his mother. She asked where they were and he told her.

She said, "Thank God! Someone just went on a rampage and shot a bunch of people at Morton's Steakhouse. I knew that was one of your favorite restaurants especially on Sunday. I just needed to make sure you and Mary were alright."

Mike grabbed Mary's hand after he hung up the phone.

"Angel, it was the Holy Spirit who told you not to go into Morton's. It was God's love that saved us from getting caught up in all that gunfire and chaos. Mary didn't know what he was talking about.

He said, "Thank you, Lord, for having mercy on us. Thank You for protecting us when we didn't even see the danger. What an awesome God you are! We love you, Lord Jesus. I praise Your mighty name." Mary smiled and silently thanked God for showing Michael how easy it was to express love to Him. She didn't think he even realized he had just praised God in his own way. It just came out like he did it all the time. When it dawns on him what just happened, he will be full of awe and joy. She hoped she would be there to see him at that moment.

Before they cleaned up the kitchen, Mary turned on the television and watched the live coverage of the killings at the steakhouse because she still wanted to know what happened. The news reporter was talking to a restaurant patron who said a man stepped into the restaurant and just waved a gun and started shooting people. The reporter asked whether the man said anything, and she said the gunman kept saying, "Today is a good day to die! He began firing his gun and continued shooting until he emptied it. When he went to reload, several of the male patrons wrestled him to the ground. They had confirmed two people dead and an unknown number were taken to local hospitals, some in critical condition. After it began to repeat, they turned it off and held hands and prayed for the victims and the gunman. They prayed for the families of the people who were killed and thanked God again for His intervention in their lives. They cleaned the kitchen and sat down to talk. Michael asked about her plans for this last week of being a single woman. She shared what she hoped would be her light schedule and he shared his. Both of them had scheduled massages; manicures; pedicures; facials; and trips to the barber. She wanted to get some new luggage. Mary kept asking about their honeymoon destination and all Michael would say was that the place had a warm climate and that she wouldn't need many clothes. Maybe a few casual dresses for dinner or dancing and some pants or shorts for touring or hiking, but not much else. For sure, she wouldn't need anything formal. When she asked how long he said at least 10 days, but probably more like 2 weeks. She wanted to try one more time to find a few casual dresses for dining and some shoes. The rest of her clothing would be items she already had. She needed a new swimming suit, but somehow, she didn't think she would really be doing that much in the water, and if she did, she figured it would probably be au natural.

Michael wanted to pick up a few things too and he kept trying to talk her into letting him come shopping with her. She kept refusing and he finally called out some number like 29. That's how many times he was going to make her pay for stuff that he was keeping track of. They had a good laugh and once the vision of the killings at the steakhouse faded from their minds, the afternoon turned out great.

He left around 9:30 and they agreed to see each other the next day. They had studio appointments as well as appointments in and around the Hartford area later in the week. Everything was going well when they heard a loud bang. They realized immediately that someone was trying to either break in his car or break the door down at Mama Lou's house. Michael told her to stay inside and to call 911. He went outside and looked, but he couldn't see anything, and his car wasn't touched. He didn't like it and neither did she. The police came and they also looked around the two houses. The neighbors had come outside but no one had seen anything. The police said they would be more visible in the neighborhood and to make sure the windows and doors were secured before retiring at night.

After that, she definitely had to make her giant leave. She gave him Mama Lou's boxes of money and he didn't even realize what it was. She asked him to put them somewhere in his house. He wanted her to go home with him, but she told him not to worry. Leave it to God. He reluctantly left but then he called her every 15 minutes until she finally told him good night and that she was not answering the phone any more. She finally settled down about midnight. The next morning, the neighborhood watch captain called to say the police apprehended two boys who had been going around scaring people just for fun. The sound was made with a tin tub, a jar and a big firecracker. Everyone was relieved that they were just teens pulling pranks in the neighborhood. However, they agreed the boys were headed down the wrong path. Everyone was glad they were caught. Mary called and gave Michael the news and he was overjoyed with relief. That afternoon, she went shopping and found three cute dresses and two swimming suits which she paid for herself. She found 2 cute pairs of sandals and several lounging sets. Satisfied, she headed to the Container Store and purchased new luggage and all the trimmings. She even bought Michael a set of the packing system components because she knew he probably didn't have any.

She was super ready to begin her life with a man who adored her and showed her in little ways as well as gigantic ways; like having the managers at Nordstrom's and Neiman's call and invite her in to get acquainted with the staff so she could select a personal sales assistant. This person would learn her style and be on the lookout for clothing and other accessories she would possibly want to purchase in order to keep her wardrobe stylish!

She had only been in those stores with Michael and was beside herself with joy at the thought of becoming a regular customer of either store, let alone both of them. He totally shot her out of the water with that surprise!

Mrs. Scott called and asked if Mary could come over Wednesday evening around seven o'clock. She wanted to go over a few things to make sure everything went smoothly on Saturday. She told her she would be there. She asked about Mama Lou and she said she had adjusted like a duck to water. Mary knew Mama Lou had a standing hair appointment and she asked to speak with her to see if she had changed it. She wasn't in. She was at Mr. Collins apartment complex. Today they took them to the movies.

Mary was surprised and extremely happy for Mama Lou. She and her companion were perfect together. Mrs. Scott told her not to worry about her. Mama Lou was going to the beauty shop with her on Friday morning and that's also when they were getting their nails done. She told Mary all she needed to think about and be doing was getting ready for Michael.

Mary smiled when she said that. She thought, *If you only knew how ready I am! I've been ready for Michael since I opened my door to him November 17th!*

February 11

Mary rang the bell at the cottage and Mama Lou opened the door and invited her in. The great room was full of women from church and the hospital and the library and the nursing home and the girls program all smiling and yelling "Surprise!" She was blown away and looked around for Mrs. Scott, who was wiping tears from her eyes. She was so proud to have gotten everyone to the cottage without her finding out.

Even without gifts, Mary had never in her life had so much fun or been the center of attention at a party. They played bride-to-be games and ate from a buffet that was constantly being replenished. The champagne flowed and she had so much fun that Mama Lou had to finally shut the party down.

Everyone was happy for Mary and looking forward to the wedding on Saturday. She didn't know she was tired until she sat down and fully relaxed. Mama Lou insisted that she spend the night with her. Mrs. Scott came in and got in the recliner and the three of them talked and giggled for hours after everyone left.

She didn't know when Mrs. Scott left the room, but when Mary woke up, Mama Lou was bringing a tray into the room with pastries, fruit, oatmeal, bacon and coffee. She enjoyed her time at the cottage and was satisfied that she and Mama Lou had been fully accepted into the family. Mary noticed that Mrs. Scott asked a lot of questions when the conversation got around to religion. She suspected that she enjoyed the ladies from Shiloh a lot more than she thought she would last night and would fit in quite well if she became a member. Mary wasn't going to mention it to her, but she was going to put it on Mama Lou's mind to invite the elder Scotts to Shiloh one Sunday. She knew that would get them there. Mary also knew that once anyone came to Shiloh and experienced true love from God's people, they would not be satisfied anywhere else. At least that's how the Shiloh congregation felt.

CHAPTER 22

February 12

Thursday was the day for getting beautiful and relaxed. The lovebirds had a wonderful day of pampering, and being photographed at various locations in and around Hartford. All they were waiting on was the wedding. They were together all day, but they made sure they were always in public.

Mary and Michael were treated to a meal with Janice and Leon that evening which they thoroughly enjoyed. She saw that the bond between the men was like that of brothers. They laughed and enjoyed pictures that Leon had from 30 years ago. They really were close in age and had known each other before the elder Scott hired him as his driver. Leon was only two years his senior. The meal was delicious and they took home carry-out plates of Lasagna, salad, garlic bread and pineapple upside cake. After the table was cleared they played bid whist.

Mary knew she had made a friend for life with Janice. She was a quiet spoken fun-loving woman who worked in a local cafeteria. She had a lovely apartment and was truly a wonderful cook. Janice asked Mary who was helping her get ready Saturday and she said no one. Janice asked if she needed her help and she immediately said yes. Mary asked her to be her guest at the rehearsal dinner also and Leon smiled and nodded. Michael was proud she invited Janice to the rehearsal dinner and to be her assistant before and after the wedding. Mary felt good too.

That evening, Mary and Janice enjoyed each other very much. Getting to know each other better, they found out their lives had taken very similar paths. They enjoyed the same things and had lived in some of the same cities, having been married to soldiers. The real cord that drew them together was their faith in God and their strong Christian beliefs. Mary had never seen Janice at Shiloh because she went to a different service. But she was an active member in the church and was fun to be around and had a lot of wisdom and faith.

Mary realized for the first time that she needed a close female friend; someone to hang out with and bounce ideas off. Someone near her own age to spend time with, and she had never had a friend like that. Looks like God had placed Janice in her path to be that friend and that made her happy.

The lovebirds reluctantly ended their day sitting in Mary's driveway for almost 30 minutes. This was next to the last night they would spend without each other and it was the hardest night for them to say goodnight.

CHAPTER 23

February 13

Friday morning began as usual, but the whole world seemed more beautiful than ever. Mary hummed while she got dressed and waited for the movers to get the last of the things going to Michael's. Everything else had been distributed to various charities and the house was empty of everything except the bedroom suit which she was giving to Janice.

She answered the door and there stood Michael, wearing the biggest smile she had ever seen on his face. He stooped and picked her up and turned around and around making Mary wonder what on earth had him so excited this morning.

"This is the last day and the last night I will ever have to spend without you in my arms! That makes me want to shout it from the roof tops."

He kissed her in the doorway and the movers who were approaching just stood on the sidewalk and clapped and whistled at this mature couple acting like kids. Mary thought about something her grandfather used to say: *'Just because there is snow on the mountain, doesn't mean there isn't fire in the valley.'* She laughed when she thought about how the men would act if they knew just how much fire *was* in the valley!

The movers were in and out in a matter of minutes. The elder Scotts were having them over for breakfast and Michael came for his bride. The meal was wonderful and filling. The atmosphere was relaxed and the conversation was all about the rehearsal dinner and the wedding. They wanted to make sure that all the logistics were set and everything was in order.

Quietly, Papa Jack left the table for a moment and returned without anyone paying him much attention. Just as quietly, Mama Dot picked up the coffee pot to refill it and returned shortly but without coffee. The elder Scotts exchanged looks and Mama Dot quietly began speaking, "Mary, I haven't known you very long and yet, I feel like God has given me the daughter I always wanted, but never had until now. You have brought so much joy into my home, and you've given me a reason to get up every day. I love you so much. I am so happy that God saw fit to give you to us; not just to Michael but to me and Jack too."

"I don't know whether you have anything old to wear tomorrow, but I would be honored if you would wear my mother's bracelet. It was given to her by her mother on her wedding day. She gave it to me the day I married Jack, and I want you to have it today on the eve of your wedding."

Mary looked lovingly at the stunning bracelet; pearls and diamonds set in white gold that looked brand new. After a few moments, she carefully put it back in the box.

She was standing when Papa Jack cleared his throat, so she sat back down.

"In all my years of knowing my son, I have never seen him smile as much, laugh as much or be as happy as he has been since you came into his life. When my family is happy, it makes me happy. I find you to be a genuine lady, in every respect. God's light in your life is evident by the way you make others feel in your presence. You make our family complete; and we never knew there was anything missing.

"I want you to have this key to our home, just like Michael has one. These are the numbers where I can be reached 24/7. You're family now, and you have full access. I love you, Mary. Welcome to the Scott family."

Mary's heart was so full she thought it might burst with love for this family. Tears freely fell from her eyes. She reached across the table and took their hands, "I am so humbled by your acts of love. I love you without hesitation. I will proudly wear your name because your son makes me happy and our love is one of a kind. God created us for each other. He must have intended for me to be your daughter, because He certainly made sure we knew he designed us for each other. I love you, Michael Scott. I love you dearly, Mama Dot and Papa Jack." Mary prayed and talked to God so beautifully until everyone was crying. Afterwards, hugs and kisses were the order of the day. It was about 11 am and everyone had things to do. Leon was picking the family up at 6:30 for the wedding rehearsal and the dinner at Shiloh. Mary thought about how blessed she was and almost got her praise on in the car. She had to pick up

Michael's ring which was going to be a surprise because he didn't know he was getting a wedding band; 18 carat gold wide band with an inscription on the inside which said, "Made and put together by God. Two sides the same body. You are Me and I am You, Forever."

When she finished all her errands she went by her house for a last look. The memories were overwhelming as she thought about William "Bill" Cross and the joy they had when they bought the house. She walked up and down her block, saying goodbye to her neighbors and promising to come back to see them. She hugged the children that were getting off the school bus. Thinking about all the memories in her neighborhood made her sad. She promised to have them over to her new home soon.

By the time she got back to the cottage, there was little time to get ready. Her children and grandchildren were meeting her at the church. She showered quickly and helped Mama Lou with her dress and jacket. Mary wore a beige and cream dress with a matching coat.

The rehearsal went well and they only needed to run through it twice. Her grandchildren who were serving as candle lighters and ushers to roll the runner down the aisle did a great job. Michael's cousins also did a good job as the flower girl and the ring bearer. What was a super surprise for Mary was that her children were in the wedding. They were standing with Mama Lou and Alford was walking her down the aisle. Michael's best men were Leon and Phillip. She was thrilled beyond words.

Of course the Shiloh family was excited to see Mary's children their families. They grew up in Shiloh and they seemed to feel right at home.

The dinner was served with lots of love to go around. Again, Mary noticed how Mama Dot seemed to be right at home. She even helped put more bread out for the tables.

James Overton stood and got everyone's attention. He welcomed Michael officially to the Shiloh family. He told Michael that he was officially a part of the Overtons' Bible study group which met every Tuesday evening at 7pm and he was expected to begin attending one week after he returned from his honeymoon. He explained that the extra week was so he could study for the next lesson. He handed him two Bible lesson books and Michael grinned from ear to ear. Everyone enjoyed his remarks and after one of the women spoke, the entire group stood and sang their church song which ended with a rousing applause and cheers. The pastor gave the benediction and everyone started leaving.

Mary and Michael kept looking at each other and grinning, both thinking about what they would probably be doing tomorrow night. They were holding hands and wishing for a few minutes of privacy when the pastor said they had less than 3 hours before they had to be away from each other. James Overton gave Michael his car keys and told Michael to bring the car back by 11:45. They were out the door in a flash.

They drove around and neither was in the mood to talk. They held hands and stared out the window both wishing it was tomorrow already. When they parked, Mary turned to Michael and he took her face in his hands and smiled before saying, "Last chance to bail out."

She replied, "Not in this life." What followed was a kiss that made the stars burst into millions pieces. They groaned as their hunger for the taste of each other was about to get out of control. From somewhere bright lights through the windows forced them apart. They were told to move along and it was nearly time to take Mary home and to get James Overton's car back.

They pulled up in front of the cottage and the windows fogged up again. Michael had rubbed the front of Mary's dress and her nipples were showing through the dress. His erection was beginning to throb and hurt.

They said goodnight and Michael didn't drive away for a few more minutes. Mary sat in the great room for a few minutes to get herself back together before going to bed. She lay awake for a long time before finally drifting off to sleep to thoughts of her and Michael making love in the sand. She suddenly remembered that tomorrow was today. She smiled and closed her eyes and drifted off to sleep.

Michael thanked James for bringing him home and waved goodbye as he pulled out of the driveway. Michael was too keyed up to sleep. He thought about texting Mary but realized it was too late. He had a beer on the porch and thought about all the changes that had occurred in his life since November 17.

He had met his soul mate and was about to be married to her; a woman who had impacted not only his life, but the lives of his parents and her surrogate mother. She had brought him into a church family that felt like he had finally made it home; he had a male friend who he genuinely liked and who was not an employee of the company. As he walked up the stairs to his bedroom, his thoughts were about this woman he loved; his woman. That thought made him smile. He kept counting all the different reasons why he loved her so much until he drifted off to sleep.

CHAPTER 24

February 14

Mary's daughters woke her up with a cup of tea and giggles. She had no idea what they were up to, but she knew it was very early on her wedding day. They climbed up in bed with her bringing with them several gift bags.

While Mary sipped on her tea, Karen began to explain what they were doing. "Well, Mama, since neither one of use could make it to the surprise bridal shower, we wanted to give you a few little things to take on your honeymoon. We are sure Daddy Mike will love them."

Mary sat her tea on the nightstand and she thanked the girls for their thoughtfulness. Then she laughed and said, "If you know he'll like them, what about me? I have to wear them. So, will I like them too?" Karen and Beverly looked at each other and started laughing. Beverly picked up the first bag and said, "Let's put it this way, if Daddy Mike likes them, we can guarantee he'll see to it that you love them."

In the first bag, Mary pulled out a little piece of red sheer fabric that was supposed to be a teddy. She was shocked, which delighted her daughters. The other gifts were a pair of black baby doll pajamas; a purple and gold t-shirt with two strategic holes in it and a pair of gold crotch-less panties; and lastly a beautiful rose colored long negligee trimmed very lightly with silver sequins and tiny pearls. It was absolutely beautiful; she knew Michael would love it!

She hugged her daughters and thanked them. They asked her what time was she planning on starting her day and she said 7 o'clock.

They said, "Oops" and tried to leave the room, but Mary said, "Oh well, since you ladies are up, why don't you bring me some toast bacon and tea."

She thought about Michael and she just had to hear his voice. Before the first ring was finished he answered, "Today is finally here my angel. Our day has come and so we will too, in a few hours," he chuckled. "I love you so much Mary that I was tempted to climb in your window last night." He laughed, "Just kidding angel."

Mary was laughing, "How did you know it was me calling? What if it had been your mother?"

"I know them" he said, "They aren't up this early and you shouldn't be either. You do know it's only 5:20 don't you? What's up? Are you just ready to get this day started? I know that's why I'm awake so early, considering it was after 1am when I went to bed."

Mary said, "My daughters had some honeymoon items for me that apparently couldn't wait for the sun to come up."

"So, where are they now? Back in bed?" Michael asked.

"I sent them to fix my breakfast since they were wide awake. Actually, Michael, I just needed to hear your voice this morning. Just think, this time tomorrow, we won't be talking on the phone or in separate beds, or separate houses. We'll be together in, where was it you said we'd be?"

He laughed, "I didn't say, Mary Elizabeth. Don't try to be slick. I'm not telling you where we're going, so stop trying to get it out of me. Hey, that makes about 37 things that I have to get you for. I'm keeping up, you know." They laughed.

They got quiet and both were thinking how blessed they were. Michael asked Mary to pray and she did. Her girls came in while she was praying and they listened to their mother talk to God about her husband to be, their marriage, their children, their friends and family and their church.

When she finished, they talked another minute and Mary noticed her daughters. She ended her call to Michael and told him she'd try to call him back before leaving for the church, if she could.

The girls got in bed with her and they all ate breakfast. It was like old times and it felt good. They talked and listened to the wisdom of their mother on love, life, family, friends and faith.

When their breakfast was finished, they asked what they could do for her. She asked them to put the new things in her luggage and Karen did. Beverly went into the bathroom and started the water for her to take a nice long bubble bath.

She had not seen their gowns so they brought them for her to see. They were beautiful soft gray gowns that were very similar to Mama Lou's. The fabric was identical but both dresses were different. Mary loved them. She knew the photographs were going to be spectacular. Mary was finished with her bath, lotioned down and creamed up before 7:30. She checked her bag containing the clothes she would wear when they left for their honeymoon. Then she checked the bag containing all the jewelry, underwear, shoes, etc. for the wedding. Then she checked to make sure she had everything packed that she wanted to take on her honeymoon. After she did this twice, she was about to make herself a nervous wreck. So she sat down and wrote thank you notes to the Scotts; Mama Lou; Janice; Leon; Phillip; the Overtons; Lois; Billie; Martha; Josie and Nellie. She was just sealing the last envelope when her phone rang.

She answered to find Michael with a smile in his voice, "You busy?"

"Never too busy for you love. "What's up?"

"Nothing" he said.

"Nothing? You called me for nothing? I don't believe you for one minute. What's on your mind Michael David Scott?"

"Well" he cleared his throat and then proceeded with what was really on his mind. "I need to ask you something Mary." He paused and Mary silently waited.

"How long will we probably have to stay at the reception?"

"Don't worry about it, giant. When the time comes for us to leave, I'll let you know, if you're not already standing by the door. Okay?"

"Okay. Look Mary, I recognize the fact that our guests won't need us to be there in order to have a good time. So after we have posed for all the photos and satisfied all the other requirements my mom has for us to do, and we've done the traditional stuff, I think we should be able to leave."

"Michael, I promise you we'll be gone before the servers come around with coffee refills. Trust me; I'm as ready for you as you are for me. This morning we'll be leaving for the church at 9:30. It won't be long sweetheart. See you at the altar. I'll be the one wearing the very big smile with stars in her eyes. See you soon my love."

As soon as the line went dead, both of them checked their watches and said, "It won't be long now. Just 90 minutes!"

Janice met Mary in the church and ushered her into the choir room which they were using as the dressing room for the bride. A floor length mirror had been brought in and a rolling clothes rack holding the bag containing her bridal gown.

The women in the bridal party were using the Fellowship Hall as their dressing room. There were mirrors and a clothes rack and four small dressing tables with stools lined up against one of the walls. The ring bearer and the flower girl was also dressing in the Fellowship Hall. The bell ringers, ushers and hostesses were using the bathrooms downstairs. The men were using the Pastors Study as their dressing area. They didn't need mirrors or racks. All the room needed was enough space for the groom to pace. He asked Leon about every 15 minutes whether he had put his bag in the limo and whether he had Mary's ring. Alford got a kick out of watching his soon-to-be step father pace back and forth. Finally, Phillip told him to sit down and drink some water; eat a peppermint. James Overton said, "Sit down man, you're making us tired just watching you." The guys jokingly agreed. Leon added, "Talk to God; read the Bible. Everything will be fine Mike, just relax please, before you give yourself a stroke."

Just then a phone rang and it was Mike's which he forgot to give to Leon, his best man.

Mary said, "Hey giant, how's it going in there?"

"Oh Baby", he said breathlessly, 'I'm about to go stir crazy in here. What am I supposed to be doing? I'm so ready for this to be over. What's taking so long?"

"Mary smiled because she knew without even seeing him that he was on the verge of giving everyone in the room a nervous breakdown, not to mention wearing down the carpet in Pastor Caldwell's office.

"Michael, sweetheart, do you love me?"

"Of course, I love you Mary. You know I love you. Why are you asking me that?"

"Because I need you to remember that I am waiting the same amount of time that you are. I need you to be calm, take deep breaths and start picturing me walking down the aisle to you. Can you see me? If you can see me, take deep breaths and smell the air for my scent. It's a new one I got just for today. While you do that, close your eyes and simply wait for me to get to you. Shortly you will kiss your wife and our new life will officially begin."

"Can you do that for me Michael? Can you sit down and close your eyes and see me? Why don't you tell God what you think about the woman you see coming to you down the aisle. I love you, Michael. Relax and wait for me. I'll be in your arms very, very soon."

He ended the call and handed Leon his phone, which he turned off and slide it into his pocket. The men watched as he sat down and relaxed, smiling with his eyes closed. The nervous energy was suddenly gone from the room and everyone relaxed and it got quiet. Phillip put a peppermint in Michael's hand and he unwrapped it and put it in his mouth.

Leon, James and Phillip looked at each other and thought the same thought, "Wow, what a woman! She sure *is* good for him. I hope he knows what just happened in here."

Alford and the preacher were thinking, "This man and this woman are so good for each other. I hope they know that God has blessed them to know just what the other one needs. It's like they read each other's minds."

For the next 20 minutes the room was filled with peace and quiet. Someone tapped on the Pastor's Study door and told them to go to their places.

They all turned to Michael who was sitting with his head bowed, resting his arms on his knees, hands clasped, eyes closed, obviously praying.

Pastor Caldwell touched him and asked him if he was ready, to which he replied, "Pastor Caldwell, I've been ready since I met my angel November 17th." He stood, wiped his eyes and blew his nose. The guys laughed at him and they checked him good and when they all agreed he looked fine, James said, "Let's go so you can get your bride."

When the doors opened and just before the bridal party began to come down the aisle, Michael looked around and nodded his approval. The church was magnificent! He was pleased with everything and he stood with his Pastor in total peace and surrender to God.

Finally, the wedding party began to enter. The candle lighters, the bell ringers, followed by the ring bearer and the flower girl. Next Beverly entered with Phillip, Karen with Leon, and lastly, Mama Lou with James Overton.

When the wedding march began and the congregation stood, Michael had his eyes glued to the door. When he caught his first glimpse of his bride, his mouth dropped open. Mary entered the sanctuary on Alford's arm and the entire congregation went "OOH".

Michael's mouth was open the entire time she walked down the aisle. He wanted to meet her before she got halfway down the aisle. The only reason he didn't move was because he was in shock and his feet were not under his control at that moment.

At that very second, in his eyes Mary was the most beautiful creature on the planet. She looked like a dream floating down the aisle. She walked the way he remembered her that first day he met her. The gown was like no other that anyone had ever seen; dark gray Chantilly lace over a satin charcoal fitted dress with horizontal ruches. Her bouquet of was silver roses, silver mesh with rhinestones on the lilies and tiny red rose buds throughout, wrapped in silver ribbon. She wore a jeweled comb with silver tipped baby's breath in her hair. She looked breathtaking. Michael didn't bat his eyes until her son put her hand in his. He didn't actually remember coming down the stairs to take her hand. Mary squeezed his hand then he smiled as he looked deeply in her eyes.

Pastor Caldwell made a brief statement that included how Michael had become a member at Shiloh and how they were going to be a beautiful couple in the church, both inside and outside. The vows they wrote were beautiful and powerful and spoke of: their love coming from their Creator who was love; they couldn't help but to love each other because He created them for each other; how blessed they were that the source of their love would never dry up and just like His love, their love was eternal.

After exchanging the rings and the final prayer, Michael saluted his bride. His mother blushed because at the exact same time, Papa Jack kissed her lovingly in the mouth in front of everyone (although no one was paying attention to the elder Scotts). When they were introduced as husband and wife, the church erupted with extended shouts of cheer and applause. All of a sudden, the organists began playing the Shiloh theme song, and those members in the audience stood and began singing. That prompted everyone else to turn to the song in the wedding program and join in.

Michael squeezed Mary's hand, and when she looked up at him he whispered, "Mary, they're holding us up! Why don't they stop?" Mary took his hand and kissed it as she whispered back, "Come on mama's grumpy baby, before you stick your thumb in your mouth." He smiled and whispered, just as the song was ending, "I can think of several things I'd rather put in my mouth right now."

They went down the aisle followed by their wedding party. When they returned, they spent about 25 minutes taking pictures. After that they were taken to Foxwoods where the next several hours were a blur of more pictures, toasts, hugs, and kisses with lots of clock watching by Michael and Mary.

They had finally made it to this day and to them they were still unable to be with each other soon enough. Finally after changing clothes and taking the long limo ride to the airport, they got in Michael's private jet where they could breathe and finally be alone.

They landed at 6:26 Connecticut time. A car was waiting and whisked them off on a rather long, bumpy road up a hillside. When they reached the top Mary was stunned speechless. She was looking at the most beautiful island villa she had ever seen. The dark green slate roof was sparkling after an island rain shower just before they arrived. God had painted a beautiful rainbow in the sky, just behind the villa. The beauty was unbelievable. The circular drive was enclosed in lush foliage and beautiful tropical flowers. The villa was almost as large as Michael's 9-bedroom house.

They were met by a dark skinned woman with a generous smile. A gentleman came down to get the luggage. The woman showed them through the house. She showed them how to get into the Jacuzzi and the private swimming pool from the bedroom without having to come through the house. She gave Michael the key and told him the kitchen was stocked as he requested and if he needed anything, to use the phone in the kitchen and someone would be happy to serve them.

The gentleman took them to the bedroom which was like something out of an island fantasy. It was simply unbelievable. There was a king size four poster mahogany bed with white sheer fabric draped all around. All of the linen was white and the sofa, loveseat and chair cushions were white. There was a flat screen TV, an armoire, and a small table with 2 chairs. The bathroom was all white marble trimmed with brushed nickel fixtures and linen closet full of white towels; bath sponges; lotions and creams of every fragrance imaginable. The shower was huge enough for four people at least, and the tub was definitely made for two people. The furniture all over the house was deep brown mahogany. The veranda furniture was dark brown wicker with white cushions. The entire place looked like it came straight out of an HGTV Magazine.

The gentleman told Michael that the car was on standby and all he had to do was call and they would bring the car right away. Michael told him to just have the car delivered tomorrow morning and to leave the keys in the ashtray.

When the newlyweds were alone at last, they began unpacking

and talking like this was what they always did on vacation. After they unpacked, they showered and put on some lounging clothes. They hugged and walked hand in hand onto the veranda. They discovered a chilled bottle of champagne in an ice bucket and two glasses. There was an ice chest containing bottled water, beer, and more champagne plus a tray containing fruit and lots of beautifully covered finger foods. Mary and Michael got comfortable snuggled on the sofa on the veranda. They sat quietly enjoying the sunset together in the privacy of their own hideaway from the rest of the world. Michael was wearing a short cotton robe. He stood up and walked to the banister looking out over the beautiful scenery, "Mrs. Scott, when you're ready to eat something, what will be your pleasure for dinner this evening? Shall we dress and go into town or shall we check out the kitchen and see what we can fix ourselves? Oh, I forgot; we can also call and have them deliver something. What are you in the mood for?" Mary stood up, stretched and then bent over and touched her toes a few times. She was wearing a yellow and green terry caftan that stopped at mid-thigh. She said, "Actually Michael, I'm still full from the reception plus the sandwich on the flight, not to mention this lovely champagne." He was thinking the same thing. He turned and walked over to Mary and said, "You know, I really just want a little something sweet, to tide me over until later."

Mary smiled and said, "Are you sure you just want a 'little' something sweet or would you like to try the full meal?"

Michael saw a sparkle in her eyes as he stepped around her and began to gather the glasses, the champagne and the tray.

"You know, the full meal idea sounds even better. I've been on a sugar diet for so long I almost forgot about all the courses that make up a good meal which are available to a hungry married man. The more I think about it, the more my appetite is calling for a full five course meal. Tonight, I want an appetizer, soup, salad, entrée, and dessert. What do you say? Are you too full to give me a five course meal this evening, Mrs. Scott?"

Michael turned toward Mary and noticed she had stopped walking and she was staring at him with a hungry look in her eyes and a smile that held him spellbound. She began floating toward the bedroom and halfway there her caftan fell to the floor. She turned around to see if Michael was looking and he was still standing in the same place looking as if he was seeing her for the very first time. In fact, he had never seen his wife's nakedness from the rear and he was almost in a trance as he watched her move. Her body made his body rigid and pulse as if setting a beat for the evening. He put everything down on the nearest table, never taking his eyes off her and moved over to her caftan on the floor.

Mary whispered, "Michael David Scott, my husband, your dinner is served". By the time she got to the bed, he was out of his robe and had her in his arms. She squealed and they tumbled over the bed hugging and laughing. When their movement stopped, they claimed the night for all eternity.

The love they made was wild, sweet and passionate. They completely gave themselves to each other. They made mad, abandoned love that had them both screaming each other's name. They made gloriously unselfish love which had them floating through the clouds while crying tears of joy. They experienced the kind of love that told Mary without a doubt she was truly in Michael's world at that moment while they alone. She had doubts about being a part of his real world once they returned home. But she would never let him know how inadequate she felt.

She lay quietly listening to their hearts beating the same rhythm. They were truly very much alike, but from totally different worlds. Just then Michael whispered softly in her ear as the sun was slowly making its way to its heavenly perch to announce the day, "I love you, Mary Elizabeth Scott."

She opened her sleepy eyes and said, "I love you, Michael David Scott. Thank you for making me a part of your world."

Michael smiled to himself and kissed her soft sweet lips, "You, are not just a part of my world. Mary Elizabeth Scott, You Are My World." They drifted into a restful, peaceful sleep in each other's arms, totally exhausted and extraordinarily happy, their hunger for each other absolutely quenched...momentarily.